The Bee Sting Deal

George Beare

The Bee Sting Deal

A
MIDNIGHT
NOVEL OF
SUSPENSE

Houghton Mifflin Company

Boston

Second Printing c

ISBN: 0-395-13942-2
LIBRARY OF CONGRESS CATALOG CARD NUMBER: 72-1848
PRINTED IN THE UNITED STATES OF AMERICA

The Bee Sting Deal

Prologue

The tanker *Atlas Monahan* was three hours out of Kuwait carrying 98,000 tons of crude oil bound for Milford Haven when she struck an unidentified submerged object. The collision tore a hole the size of a house in her, and her forward tanks, holding altogether 20,000 barrels of crude, spewed their cargoes into the sea and laid an oil slick on the soft, green surface of the Persian Gulf that eventually spread out ten miles long behind her and half a mile wide on either side of her.

Immediately the collision occurred, her master had her thrown into full astern; even so, from full ahead to a dead stop, she made headway for a further eighteen miles, such is the momentum of such tonnage multiplied by thirteen knots. By then it was out of the question for the stricken ship to go about and return to the scene of the accident and look for whatever it was that she had hit. But whatever it had been, it had had no business being there, uncharted and un-notified in the middle of one of the busiest shipping lanes on earth.

The tanker now crept on down the Gulf at dead slow, her after bilges flooded in an effort to raise the great, jagged rent in her bows clear of the sea. Some tugs came out from Sitra, where the Bahrain Petroleum Company's oil terminal is, to bring the *Atlas Monahan* in.

They moored her at the island wharf. This is a group of huge pylons sunk in the sea-bed supporting a number of gantries through which are run the six-inch diameter hoses that bring the crude and refined products of the company from the mainland of Bahrain several miles away,

5

out across the shallows to where there is enough depth for the big tankers to come in and take on cargo. Here, at low tide, the *Atlas Monahan*'s keel rested on the bottom. The dregs that remained in her bow tanks, a crude oil-sea water mix, were pumped out so that her forrard end lifted in the four-inch-thick metal plating of her leading edge was raised above the waterline.

Thus she sat back on her rudder at the island on the morning Victor Stallard brought his boat, *Sandman*, down to Sitra to bunker.

The *Sandman* was forty-three feet long and powered by twin Perkins diesels, and Stallard operated her on behalf of any big-game fishermen, skin-divers, sight-seers, or tourists who could pay his charter. She was luxuriously equipped and air-conditioned, the way rich men like their boats to be, and she could move at almost thirty knots when pressed. Besides the *Sandman*, Stallard had other strings to his bow, but the *Sandman* represented the only one at which he could labour openly and in public. His other enterprises were carried on, mostly, after dark.

Bringing her down from Manama in the north, he sat in the high, swivel arm chair behind the wheel in the cockpit wearing just a canvas hat, sun-glasses, and faded jeans sawn off below the knees, and his body, deeply tanned, glistened and dripped with sweat. It was a hundred and thirty degrees Fahrenheit in the shade. Coming into Sitra, he got his first, and indeed his only, look at the *Atlas Monahan*.

Her gigantic upthrust bows blotted out a whole segment of the deep blue sky, and the great hole below her Plimsoll line put him in mind of the snapping jaws of a monstrous, rearing shark.

He swung the *Sandman* alongside the bunker barge moored on Sitra Wharf across the water about a quarter of a mile from the island where the tanker lay. His crewman Ali, and the Arab operators on the barge, made her fast and set about fuelling her up. Stallard mopped himself

6

down with a towel, put on a shirt, and climbed up the ladder to the wharf. He walked along the heavy planking, stepping over bunches of pipe and skirting piles of barrels, to the office of the wharf superintendent, whose name was Musa Gafour. Inside the office, the air-conditioning made for blessed respite and Stallard's sweat-soaked shirt froze against his back. Musa Gafour looked up from his desk.

'Come to settle your account?' he asked.

Stallard smiled. 'Get stuffed,' he said, politely.

The Arab grinned at him and rose from his chair. 'Coffee?' he asked.

'Please,' Stallard nodded.

The percolator bubbled and hissed on its stand on the wide window-ledge behind the desk. Musa Gafour poured two cups. On the rail of the wharf, visible through the window, a huge sign in English and Arabic said: NO SMOKING. Beyond the rail, out across the limpid sea, was the island wharf, and the great holed tanker moored against it.

'What happened to her?' Stallard asked, nodding towards the island.

'She hit a whale,' Musa Gafour said.

'You're kidding,' Stallard said, accepting the mug of coffee the Arab handed him.

Musa Gafour shrugged. 'That's the official explanation,' he said.

'Whose official explanation?'

'The navy's.' The Arab sat down again behind his desk, placing his coffee cup on the blotter pad in front of him. 'Some whale, huh?'

'Some whale indeed.' Stallard was still standing at the window, looking out across the water at the *Atlas Monahan*. 'Where did it happen?'

'Off Djezirat, two days ago. With fifty fathoms under her, so it sure wasn't coral.'

'Must have been a sub,' Stallard said.

'Oh no, my friend. It was a whale.'

Stallard looked back grinning at the Arab's sarcasm.

Musa Gafour went on, 'Even now they are up there trying to rescue this whale.'

'Who are up where?'

'Up at Djezirat, where the collision occurred. The Americans have got a frigate up there, and the Royal Navy has gone up with a diving tender. They are, you understand, extremely concerned about this whale.'

'As you say,' Stallard observed, 'it must be some whale.'

'And as you say,' the Arab said, putting down his coffee, 'it must be a sub.'

Stallard came back around the desk and sat in the chair in front of it. On the opposite wall, above a filing cabinet, hung a calendar with a large nude on it. Miss July. 'If it was a sub,' he said, 'whose was it? I didn't know they had any subs in the Gulf.'

'They haven't. At least, the British and the Americans haven't.'

'So it must have been Russian?' Stallard asked, somewhat preoccupied with gazing at Miss July's breasts.

Musa Gafour shrugged. 'Could have been French.'

'What would the French want up here?'

'What would the Russians want up here?'

'Your calendar?'

'I heard a theory advanced last night,' the Arab said, 'that the tanker wasn't in collision. She was torpedoed. They actually hit her with a dummy torpedo, just to hole her and spill some of her cargo. She's lost about twenty thousand barrels of crude, I'm told. That means one hell of a big oil slick is floating around out there in the Gulf, and that means there will be one hell of a lot of dead fish underneath it. As you know, Vic, all these people around the Gulf live on fish; so that oil slick is not going to enhance the local view of the Western oil companies.'

After a moment, Stallard said, 'That's ridiculous.'

'Why?'

'They're not going to send a nuclear submarine out here just to try to make the name of the oil business stink a little bit higher than it already stinks.'

8

'Why do you say "nuclear"? Why must it be a nuclear submarine?'

'Because it would have to remain submerged for weeks, to get in and out of here unobserved.'

The Arab nodded, slowly. 'Of course,' he murmured, and then sipped some coffee. Then he said, 'Then it is probably armed, with missiles, with nuclear warheads.'

'That's if it's a submarine,' Stallard said.

'If it is a submarine,' the other man said, looking back across his shoulder, through the window, and across the water to the *Atlas Monahan*, 'and it made that hole—I wouldn't give much for the chances of the poor bastards aboard it.'

At that moment, the door opened and the head man from the bunker barge came in with some papers on a clip-board. He handed the clip-board to Stallard who looked at the docket and observed that the *Sandman* had taken on one hundred and forty-three U.S. gallons of Derv. Ali had made his mark beside the amount to indicate that he had checked the levels with the dipsticks and the head man was not trying to pull a fast one. Stallard signed it and handed it over to Musa Gafour.

'How much do I owe you now, anyway?' he asked the wharf superintendent.

'Around eight hundred dollars for fuel,' Musa Gafour said, 'and about twenty-five for coffee.'

'Let me know when it's a thousand,' Stallard said, and finished his coffee.

The Arab grinned. 'Cheers, Vic,' he said. 'And watch out for submarines, huh?'

'I'll try to avoid them,' Stallard smiled.

9

1

This newspaper office, at 5.30 a.m., was as dead as Tutankhamen. The last edition had gone to bed an hour and a half ago; the good scribes who had written it were home in bed with their wives, the bad scribes, which was most of them, were around the corner in the Press Club washing the taste of printer's ink out of their mouths. Cynthia wished she could join them; but the Press Club does not admit women.

Her escort of the previous evening, the Honourable Bertrand Baverstock, stood to one side of her and watched her with a kind of chinless, weary displeasure while, in silence, she contemplated the great editorial floor of the *Daily World*.

The thousand telephones and typewriters and teleprinters were now strangely silent, and every level surface was littered with paper; screwed-up, defaced, ruined, wasted paper. Cups stood with cold dregs of coffee congealing amid the tons of yesterday's cigarette butts. At the far end of the room, something moved, like a squirrel on the floor of the forest. a charlady with a mop and a bucket.

Cynthia Godwin opened the door of the news-editor's office, went in, and sat behind the news-editor's desk. She looked up, with her cold, deep emerald-green eyes, across the shrouded electric typewriter, at the Honourable Bertrand, who loitered like a whipped cur, not understanding, in the open doorway. Earlier, his evening dress had been impeccable, but now it was somewhat creased; his eyeballs were red, and a shadow had appeared about his hitherto brilliantly barbered jaw.

'What on earth, Cynthia, are we doing here?' he inquired.

'I work here,' she said, dully.

'But surely not at 5.30 a.m., ole gel,' he pleaded.

She opened a drawer. The bottle was where it should have been, and she took it out of the drawer and placed it on the desk. Then she nodded towards the water fountain, beneath which a box of waxed paper cups was housed. 'Pass me a cup,' she told Bertrand. 'Two, if you want one.'

'Want one,' he said, passing across two cups. 'I need one.'

She poured them each a generous slug.

About a year ago, the Honourable Bertie had been legally cut adrift from his fourth wife and he had been hoping to make Godwin his fifth. That hope had been dashed about a week ago, when he had put it to her.

'Marry you!' she had exclaimed. 'Bertie, I wouldn't pee on you if you were on fire.'

At least now he knew where he stood.

Last evening they had been to a party, which had been somewhat of a bore, then to the Beachcomber, which was one of Bertie's haunts. It was there that she had received a phone call, and after it, her mood had altered. From the happy, stinging bitchiness that he loved, she had gone dark and sour.

'Here's to Tod Spencer,' she said, and raised her paper cup.

'Cynthia,' Bertie said with feeling, 'what was the phone call about?'

She swallowed some whisky. 'Him,' she said. 'Tod Spencer.'

'Who is Tod Spencer?'

'Who *was* Tod Spencer,' she corrected. 'He *is* no longer. He was murdered early this morning. That's what the phone call was about.'

'Oh dear!' Bertie said, and frowned.

'Got a light?' she asked, placing the filter-tip of a cigarette between her teeth.

Bertie foraged under his overcoat, down into his trousers pocket, and produced a lighter. 'He was a friend,' Bertie said, 'I take it.'

She nodded, looking at the now burning tip of her cigarette. Overhead, the fluorescent light tubes hummed, acid white. 'This was his office we're sitting in,' she said. 'This was his chair I'm sitting on.' She raised her paper cup. 'And this was his booze we're drinking. So, here's to him.'

The man frowned, and looked down at the floor. 'Do you have to be so damned morbid?' he asked, rhetorically.

She laughed. Then she said, 'I'm almost tempted to marry you, Bertie. You're a million bloody laughs.'

The Honourable Bertrand looked up, angry and hurt. 'You were very close to this Spencer, presumably,' he accused.

She shrugged. 'We just did the same job together for ten or twelve years. He taught me. Everything I know about journalism, he taught me.' Her jaw tightened and the widow's peak to her chin sharpened. The green eyes disappeared behind fences of black lash. At length she said, 'They phoned me, because they wanted me to write a tribute.'

'Why didn't you?'

'Because I was so damned drunk I couldn't spell my own name, let alone his.' Then she laughed again, the eyes flashing vibrantly green at him.

He stood at the glass partition that enclosed the small office, looking out across the vast wasteland of the editorial room. There was a number of charladies at work there now. At length, over his shoulder, he asked, 'What were the circumstances?'

'Pour me another drink,' she said, and placed her paper cup on the desk beside the typewriter.

'Well?' he prompted, pouring the drink.

'I don't know,' she said, shrugging irritably. 'They found him in his flat. He lived above a betting shop in Soho.' She looked up and chuckled at the improbability of the address. 'He'd been roughed up, and'—she frowned, pre-occupied—'and he had been stabbed in the heart with some-thing with a blade like a sabre . . .'

'Good heavens,' Bertie whispered. 'Do they have any idea who . . .'

Abruptly, she swallowed her drink, stubbed out her cigarette, and stood up. Of course they had no idea who. . . . as Bertie had put it. Neither did she. But she did have an idea why, and she had also an idea about who might be next on the list. Suddenly, she was very frightened.

'Take me home, Bertie,' she said.

'Yes, please,' Bertie said, with alacrity.

She took the Scotch bottle out into the editorial room and waved it aloft at the charladies. 'Mesdames!' she yelled.

The charladies looked up from their toil.

Godwin asked them, 'May I interest you in what remains in this flagon?'

'You may indeed,' one of them said.

Placing the bottle on the nearest desk, Godwin said, 'Then swallow it fast and bury the bottle.'

'Ta, luv,' one of the charladies said.

Going down in the elevator, Godwin said to Bertie, 'Tributes my backside. That was the best thing I could have done for poor old Tod now. Protect his good name and hide the bottle.'

'You mean that that is why we came down here to Fleet Street? Just to dispose of that damned bottle?'

She looked pained. 'He drank a lot,' she said. 'It would have looked bad.' Then she said, 'Bertie, you won't mind if I get a taxi?'

'I will. I'll drop you off.'

'Then you won't mind if I don't ask you in?' she said.

'No,' he said. 'I suppose I won't mind.'

'Bertie,' she said, as they walked around the building to the car-park, 'you're a brick.'

He opened the door and let her into the passenger seat of the Aston Martin. She sat back in the luxurious car as

Bertie headed it west, towards Kensington where she lived. He really was a brick, she thought. A true gentleman. A gentleman who would believe all her lies knowing them to be lies, and pander to all her ridiculous whims. Those swines who got Tod Spencer would not believe lies, and, quite obviously, Tod had died rather than tell them the truth. Who had he been protecting? Mrs Black? Probably, Godwin reckoned.

This had been the night they got Tod. This night, in years to come, would be made a stepping-stone in time. The night Tod Spencer was murdered. Was there going to be another such milestone, Godwin wondered. Was tomorrow going to be the day Cynthia Godwin got hers?

Bertrand Baverstock was a gentleman, but the man Godwin wanted with her right now was not. Her mind went back to days of blazing heat and the stench of sweat in the Persian Gulf at high summer, a big man who moved slowly, because he knew the heat, but deliberately, and with a knife-edge to his purpose. His name was Victor Stallard. Should she cable him? He was five thousand miles away. Would he come? He would not pander to any of her ridiculous whims; but she knew that if she was in trouble, he would come.

She would cable him immediately, from the flat, phone it through—better still, why not phone him direct, in Bahrain? No, he might be at sea. Better to cable it, then they would contact him by radio if he were out.

'Darling,' Bertie said.

The car had stopped. She was home. And now the dread returned. She put her hand on his arm. 'Bertie. I'm sorry for what I said. Come up with me.'

'Darling, I want to go to bed,' Bertie said, long-sufferingly.

'You can't go to bed without your breakfast, Bertie. Come up with me.'

There was a certain demand in her attitude that made him realise, then, that more than his breakfast was on her

15

mind. 'Are you scared of something?' he asked.

'Yes,' she said.

'What?'

'The dark.'

He smiled and looked back through the rear window. Back there, across the roof-tops of London, dawn was breaking. 'But it is no longer dark,' he said. ' "But, soft! what light through yonder window breaks?" '

Anyway, she thought, if killers did wait in her flat, of what the hell use would Bertie be? She would only get him killed as well as herself.

But how *could* they be up there? Why *should* they be waiting for her? She had not been to see Mrs Black. Not yet, anyway. And Tod Spencer had not told them anything; that was why Tod Spencer was dead. But whoever had done for Tod must surely have known that he had worked for the *Daily World*, and that Cynthia Godwin had been his understudy. That is what frightened her.

Then Bertie got out of the car. 'Come on then,' he said, an uncharacteristically businesslike snap in his voice that informed her his patience was almost exhausted.

Her groundless fears were trying even Bertie's undying love.

The fact was that whether Tod Spencer had talked or not, they, whoever they were, would have had to kill him.

By now she was pretty certain that they, whoever they were, were waiting for her in her flat on the fifth floor of this building. She got out of the car and stood looking at Bertie, who extended his right hand to her.

'No,' she said. She had behaved abominably for Bertie, she could not ask him to do this for her.

Bertie screamed, 'My good God in Heaven, woman!' Then he controlled his wobble. 'I'm coming up with you. Now come on, I will suffer no more bloody nonsense.'

'Bertie, I'm telling you, I don't want you to come up.'

'Oh *hell*!' Bertie expleted.

'Please go,' she said.

16

'Cynthia,' he said, and then looked at her, seriously, for a moment. After the moment, he said, 'You are, in some way, involved in the affairs of this man Spencer, who was murdered tonight. Are you not?'

'Only insofar as I worked with him.'

'But you fear the fate that he suffered—presumably for the same reason as he suffered it. Am I right?'

'I'm just scared.'

'And you think that the people who killed him are waiting for you in your apartment.'

'Oh, Bertie,' she said, 'please go.'

'How can I go and leave you in this predicament?'

'Bertie, I'm not going to marry you,' she said, 'even if you give your life for me.'

'That was what our English master used to call an "Irishism". But I have no intention of giving my life for you. Just let me ring the police. There's a phone-box at the end of the street.'

'No,' she said.

'Why not?'

'Because I think that you'll get me murdered for certain if you involve the police.'

Bertie sighed.

The chill of dawn was in the air and Godwin shivered. 'Oh, come on then,' she said, and turned and mounted the steps to the building.

As they were going up in the elevator, she suddenly grinned and said to him, 'You wouldn't be doing this if you were sober.'

'Oh no?' Bertie asked, pompously.

'Never mind,' she consoled him. 'You may not live to suffer the hangover.'

Inside the building, it was still dark, but no light shone from under the door of Godwin's apartment, which was encouraging. She inserted the key in the lock and opened the door. With a downward flick of her right hand she switched on the living-room lights, and entered. The room

17

was unoccupied and in exactly the state in which she had left it yesterday afternoon.

Bertie, audibly, exhaled.

Godwin said to him, 'You look in the bedroom and the bathroom, I'll look in the kitchen.'

'Oh Christ,' Bertie whispered; but they searched the place thoroughly, looked under the bed, in the wardrobes and the airing cupboard, opened the french windows and looked on the balcony, and there was no sign of killers.

Bertie flopped on the leather settee. 'Is the door locked?' he asked.

She went to the door and locked it. 'Yes,' she said.

'Now, darling,' he said, 'tell me, please, why you won't have the police.'

'Bertie,' she said, and patted him on the shoulder, 'make some coffee, will you? I've got to send a cable.' She went to the phone.

Bertie left at about eight o'clock. So much had happened to him in the preceding twelve hours that he fluffed his departure speech. 'You realise that I've taken my hands in my life for you this morning?'

'Yes, darling, of course I realise it,' she said.

'Will I see you again, Cynthia?'

'Of course you will. Ring me.'

He put out his mouth to be kissed, and she kissed it, and then he went. As she was closing the door, it seemed to jam against something. She opened it a little to see what the obstruction was, and there was a man standing there. He was the obstruction.

He was a short, thickly built man with a blazing red face and silvery white hair, who carried a thick, bamboo cane like a swagger-stick under his left arm. 'Good morning, Miss Godwin,' he smiled, and she felt the door being eased gently but firmly back as, unbidden, he entered. 'May we come in?'

'We?' she whispered, hoarsely, stupidly, and looked up.

Two more men now stood in the doorway. They were coming in and she could offer them no resistance. As the

18

last of them closed the door behind him, locked it, and dropped the key into his jacket pocket, she experienced a sensation like a cold claw closing tight inside her belly.

The short man's companions were both about six feet four and broad of shoulder. One had dark hair done in a prison crop so short the white dome of his scalp showed bare. The other had long, luxurious blond locks, flowing and waving and set, obviously, by a women's hairdresser. But both of these men had the flat, hard pulped visages of fighters and, under bald and leavened brows, the dull, insensitive eyes of beasts.

The short man was sweating slightly. He must have come up the stairs rather than the elevator, and he took from his breast pocket a wine-red handkerchief with which he sponged his broad forehead. His white hair was cut the Army way, short back and sides, with tiny white spikes of it peppering the back of the crimson, bull neck which was cratered by small-pox or carbuncles. The hair sprouted stiff as tooth-brush bristles around the sides of his head and thinned out to nothing on top, revealing a shining pink pate.

'My name is Davies,' he said, his voice like a car tyre running on gravel. 'Colonel John Davies. These men are my assistants. I don't know whether you had the same sinking feeling or not, but we were beginning to fear that Bertie was never going to leave.'

Godwin could not speak. She stood staring in fascinated horror at this man whose mouth opened and closed as he spoke like the parting of two blades against a powerful spring and whose eyes were bright, pagan blue.

Uninvited, he sat down. He made himself comfortable in one of her large, black leather arm chairs, and crossed his legs. He wore a pale beige, tropical weight suit, and, on a dark, wine-red shirt, an old school tie she fancied she recognised as Sandhurst.

'Who are you?' Godwin whispered.

Colonel Davies did not answer. He sat loosely holding the bamboo cane, gazing back at her. The cane moved

19

slightly as he rotated it in his large, red hands the backs of which were covered in curled ginger hair. On the short, stubby little finger of the left hand was a ring of massive gold bearing a slate-coloured stone.

At length he said, 'I've told you who I am, Miss Godwin.'

'But what are your credentials? Whom do you represent?'

'I would like a drink,' he said quietly. 'Scotch, if you don't mind. Neat.'

Scotch, at 8.30 a.m., she mused. A kindred spirit.

On his feet he wore yellow suède desert boots, scuffed and worn shiny where his feet were bunched against the insides of them. He gently tapped one end of the cane, now, against the side of one of the boots. She observed that the cane was comprised of two separate pieces; there was a smooth crack around the shaft about four inches from one end, giving it the appearance of a rather fancy bicycle pump. 'Just get the drink, will you?' he said.

Godwin swallowed to clear a constriction in her throat. She was aware of the short man's 'assistants', who stood behind her at either end of the settee. Silently, they just stood there. She went to the liquor cabinet and poured about four fingers of Queen Anne into a leaded glass tumbler and handed it to Davies.

'Thank you,' he said. 'Now sit down. Over there, where I can see you.'

He had taken a cigar from inside his jacket, and he fingered it unlit, absently, watching her. She was wearing a white cocktail dress which exposed her long, slender legs right up to the hips, and as she sat on the settee she was conscious of his caressing eyes, like the eyes of a snake seeking a tender place to bite.

Now he was lighting the cigar, his eyes, hooded, watching the flaring match at the tip of it. He opened his mouth and smoke came out of it. 'Miss Godwin,' he said, 'have you ever heard of the codeword Bee Sting?'

She looked at him and blinked. 'The what?'

'Bee Sting!' he repeated, suddenly leaning forward in his chair, his eyes drilling her. 'The Bee Sting Deal, Miss Godwin.'

'No,' she said. 'I've never heard of it.'

The red-faced man leaned back, wearily, in the big chair. He sipped whisky and, for some moments, drew thoughtfully on his cigar. Then he said, softly, 'You are aware, Miss Godwin, of what happened to your colleague Tod Spencer earlier this morning.'

Yes, she was aware. She tried to say yes, she was aware, but that constriction was back in her throat. Terror had seized her larynx. Like a puppet, she nodded her head.

'So you know what will happen if you lie to me,' Davies said, and she watched in horror as he drew, from the bamboo cane, a stiletto blade at least twelve inches long. Tod Spencer had been stabbed in the heart with something with a blade like a fencing sabre . . . Davies returned the blade within the shaft of the cane and screwed up the handle.

'I swear to you,' she croaked, 'I've never heard of this Bee Sting thing!'

'All right,' Davies said, and ashed his cigar on the carpet, 'we'll try a different tack. How do you suppose Mr Spencer came to hear of it?'

'I have no idea,' she said. But she did have an idea. Spencer must have heard of it from Mrs Black, and that, she now realised, was the information Spencer had died rather than divulge. She felt a violent emotion rise up her gorge almost to choke her, and tears blurred her vision.

She screamed at Davies: 'You murdering bastard!'

Calmly, the man addressed one of his assistants. 'Get her a drink.'

The blond one moved to the liquor cabinet.

'Take a drink, Miss Godwin,' Davies advised, like a doctor at her bedside. 'It will compose you.'

Suddenly, fury gripped her.

The assistant handed her a tumbler half full of whisky; but she was so full of hate she trembled and the spirit slopped over the glass. The assistant reached to steady her hand, and she flung the contents of the glass in his face. At the impact of the liquor against his eyeballs, the man blinked, and she shied the empty glass at Davies. Davies ducked. The glass bounced off the back of the chair where his head had been resting, and the big, blond assistant brought his left fist through at the end of a short-arm jab to Godwin's breast-bone that felled her like a poleaxed steer.

She curled up in the shape of a foetus on the carpet, retching and convulsing, in agony to draw breath, which, when it came, transfixed her chest like a white-hot spear. A hand gripped her by the hair and she felt the hair tearing out of her scalp; she scrabbled stupidly to rise, to stand, to go with the hand tearing her hair. She was screaming. Then something like a cricket bat smashed her across the mouth, cutting the scream off.

Her mouth was full of blood. Standing uncertainly, suspended by the hair, she was mistily aware of Davies in front of her, shorter than she was, of the bold scarlet blaze of the face, of the cigar in the right hand and the left hand, stubby and globular, with that ring of noble gold adorning the little finger, reaching out to grip the top of her dress, and then whipping back, ripping the dress from her body.

Her hair was released. She stood in white briefs and a small bra, her arms, maiden-aunt-like, crossed over her breasts, her head hanging forward and long threads of blood and spittle falling from her loose lips.

'No more drama, Miss Godwin,' she heard Davies saying, 'or you really will get hurt.'

Then he pushed her gently and she flopped back on the settee. One of the assistants had gone into the bathroom and brought back a towel for her. She covered her mouth with it, and spat into it.

Davies said, 'Give her the drink again.'

The assistant poured another drink and gave it to her.

Davies had resumed his chair. 'There is no need to get worked up,' he said, solicitously. 'I believe you. You really

22

don't know where Spencer got his information.'

She shook her head and then took a long draught of whisky. It was like a mouthful of Prussic acid, but she swallowed it, and when she spoke it was as if she had a tennis ball in her mouth. 'I don't know,' she said to Davies.

'But you can find out,' he said.

She looked at him.

The Colonel got up from the chair and paced the floor, his whisky and cigar in his right hand. 'Last night,' he said, 'about midnight, Tod Spencer turned up at Belgravia, at the home of Mr and Mrs Conrad Hasseler, of whom you may have heard. Their daughter, Sigrid, has been in the news recently, she went missing about a week ago in France, kidnapped or something. There's a police search on for her, all over Europe.'

'I know about Sigrid Hasseler,' Godwin said. 'She's in all the papers.'

'Well, last night, as I say,' the man continued, 'Spencer turned up at this girl's parents' home, and demanded to know from them what was the Bee Sting Deal. Now I want to know from you, Miss Godwin, who told Spencer about the Bee Sting Deal, and why he should connect it with the Hasselers.'

'But how can I find out?' she asked. 'If you hadn't killed him . . .'

'If you really put your heart and soul into it, my dear, you can find out,' Davies said. 'You've worked with Spencer for years. You know his contacts, how he operated, what he was working on, you have access to his office, his notes, his friends, his associates. You can find out.' The blue eyes focussed her, rock still, hooded by sagging pads of flesh. 'You have eight hours,' he said. 'There is no point in going to the police, the police can't touch me. There is no point in seeking help from any other agency, and that includes your father; I know he is Lord Godwin of Carrick, and a powerful man in this country; but not even he can protect you against me. The commission with which I am charged is far more important than your life, or Tod

23

Spencer's life, or any other individual's life, and nothing is going to impede me. So if by five o'clock this afternoon you are still unable to tell me what I want to know, I'm afraid you are going to suffer the same fate as Mr Spencer.'

She sat numbly, staring at him.

'I'll be in touch,' he said, and his assistants followed him to the door. The one who had the key unlocked the door and left the key in it.

For a while after they had gone, Godwin sat on the settee and shivered, violently, from shock.

2

She had sent a cable to Stallard in Bahrain unaware of the fact that at the time she sent it, Stallard was in an aircraft thirty-five thousand feet over the Dardanelles, heading for London. His estimated time of arrival there was 1330 hours G.M.T. The job had come up the previous afternoon and entailed his departure for London on the first available flight, and as he expected to be there only a matter of hours it seemed hardly worthwhile interrupting Godwin's day by having her meet him at the airport. He did intend to phone her later, when he was more certain of his movements.

He travelled first-class because somebody else was paying. Also because he needed the leg-room; he was a big man and tended to lie rather than sit in a seat. Airplanes made him nervous, bored him, and frustrated him, and after a long flight like this one of eight or nine hours, he would invariably disembark in a foul humour unless he had been receiving first-class attention throughout. Here, the whisky was free and he was making the most of it. Although, as the stewardess observed, he did hold it well.

The stewardess knew him; she had slept with him once on an overnight stop over in Bahrain; but he had done her the courtesy, throughout this flight, of pretending that they had never previously met. For this she was grateful, and hoped fervently that he would be available on her next stopover in Bahrain. On the occasion of their first encounter he had been attired in a pair of well-worn dungarees, desert boots, a sweat shirt, and four days' growth of beard. This time, he wore a perfectly cut charcoal grey suit, blue shirt, and a dark tie; but he was still Stallard of the deeply lined, deeply tanned, craggy face, the close-cropped, grey-peppered black hair, and the pale blue eyes ever ready to go hard as nails on you if you displeased him.

There was just one thing wrong with him, the stewardess decided. He would insist on smoking these great, long, crooked, black, Mexican cheroots which were stinking out the whole cabin.

As he was disembarking at Heathrow he gave the stewardess a small smile. She said, 'I hope you've enjoyed your flight, sir, and that we'll be flying together again.'

He nodded and said softly, 'Thank you.'

She smiled back, tight-lipped and starry-eyed, and watched him go.

From the airport he took a taxi into London, to the Dorchester Hotel. He deposited his bag with the porter there and, at the reception desk, asked to be shown to the suite of Mr Jamil Bazarki.

Bazarki was waiting for him, a tall, olive-skinned, slender Arab, a native of the island of Jarma, which lies about twenty-seven miles off the coast of Iran in the Persian Gulf. Jamil Bazarki was in fact the man appointed by the Ruler of Jarma, to represent the island in the Iranian Parliament at Teheran, and so, in a sense, you could have said that Jamil Bazarki was a Member of Parliament. But his income was about twenty-five times that of even the best set-up Member of the British Parliament.

Jamil Bazarki had two loves in life, his work and his yacht. The latter was, as Stallard recalled from a visit he had made aboard her in the Gulf some years ago, a 175-foot, 300-ton floating palace named *Shaheen*. For some months now, the yacht had been undergoing a refit at Hamburg, and it was in connection with this that Stallard had been summoned so hastily from Bahrain.

'Thank you for coming at such short notice,' Bazarki said to him, and shook his hand. In the lounge of the hotel suite, another man was waiting. He was very neat, exquisitely tailored and barbered, and of middle age, but without any fat on him at all. He had cold, grey eyes and rather full, red lips in an almost anaemic white face. His slick blond hair was receding from a high domed forehead.

'Victor Stallard,' Bazarki said, 'this is Conrad Hasseler.'

Hasseler remained seated, lying back, his legs crossed, one arm along the back of the settee, gazing lazily up at the two men standing before him.

'Hello,' Stallard said to him.

'I believe my wife knows you,' Hasseler said. His voice was as lazy, soft, and pale as the rest of him.

'How come?' Stallard asked.

'Virginia. She gets around quite a bit in the Gulf.'

'Maybe she knows me,' Stallard said, 'but I can't remember having met her.'

Hasseler grinned, but not with his eyes. 'I'm sure she won't be flattered to hear that,' he said.

'Are you the Hasseler whose daughter is missing on the Continent?' Stallard asked.

'Yes,' the other man said, curtly, and looked away to indicate that he did not wish to pursue that topic.

In case Stallard should pursue it, Bazarki broke in, quickly, 'You know, of course, Victor, that Mr Hasseler is President of the Greenhalgh Banking Company, who loaned us the money to pay for our share of the Jarma Causeway, connecting the island of Jarma with the mainland of Iran.'

'No,' Stallard admitted, 'I didn't know that.'

'He will, of course, be one of Jarma's distinguished guests on the bridge of *Shaheen* when the causeway is ceremonially opened in a month's time. So will you, Victor, if, of course, you can get her there on time.'

26

Stallard smiled. 'That depends on the Atlantic Ocean,' he said.

'What will you have to drink?'

'Black coffee,' Stallard said, and sat in a chair facing Conrad Hasseler across a wide, glass-topped coffee table.

Jamil Bazarki sat next to Hasseler on the settee. He lit a cigarette while the boy was pouring coffee, and then he said, 'You probably know all this already, Vic, but I'll make my little speech anyway. The Jarma Causeway has taken four years to build. It is thirty-two point seven-eight miles long and it cost a hundred and twenty million dollars. Of this sum, the Iranian Government put up sixty-six and two-thirds per cent, and the Jarma Government the remaining third, forty million dollars, the surety for which is the Greenhalgh Banking Company, to wit: our friend Mr Hasseler here. The Persians wanted us, they were prepared to pay eighty million dollars to get us, and now they have us. We have no oil, we have no water, we are a very poor state indeed; but what we have is a natural, deep-water harbour. The only one in the Gulf, and with our harbour, and a continuous supply of super-tankers, the Persians can ship four times more oil per year out of the Gulf than Kuwait, Saudi, Qatar, Abu Dhabi, and the rest of them put together. For our part, Jarma is coming under the dominion of a rich kingdom, but one which is democratically and decently governed. We are going to have schools and hospitals. We are going to have release from ignorance, and freedom from fear of disease. And, now, finally, after years of bickering and—"negotiating" —we have this causeway, an engineering miracle which has been described as the eighth wonder of the modern world, an umbilical cord binding us to a new mother, a road across the sea. Jarma's road into the future.'

At the end of his speech, Bazarki stubbed out his cigarette and took a sip of coffee. His hands were trembling. As an M.P., Stallard reckoned, the Arab lacked nothing.

Also sipping coffee, Stallard asked, 'And what exactly is the problem with the yacht?'

'No problem at all,' Bazarki said. 'As you know, she's been in Hamburg for a refit and new engines. This work is now complete, and she'll be cleared for sea on Friday. The trouble is, the contractors have had such marvellous weather in the Gulf that they've been able to hand over the causeway six weeks ahead of schedule, and the opening ceremoney, at the request of the Persians, has been brought forward a month. They, understandably, want to start using it as soon as possible. It will now be opened one month from next Friday, and for the occasion I desperately want to have the yacht there. Had they had the original two months to get her there, I'd have trusted my own skipper and crew. But, with the Suez closed, and having to go round the Cape and get her there inside the month, I'd prefer to have a more professional hand on the helm. So I've called for you.'

'What will she do?' Stallard asked.

'The Germans assure me, nearly forty knots,' Bazarki said, proudly. 'She'll outrun a destroyer.'

Stallard smiled. 'She'll outrun *some* destroyers,' he corrected.

For Hasseler, the waiter had not only to pour the coffee but to pick up the cup off the coffee table and hand it to him.

'And the crew?' Stallard asked of Bazarki.

'You know my skipper, Andreas.'

Stallard nodded, sipping coffee. 'Andreas the Greek,' he said.

'He's a good seaman,' Bazarki allowed, 'but most of his professional experience has been gained in wheeling pleasure craft around the Mediterranean and the Arabian Gulf. He doesn't know the Atlantic. This is why I've called you in. There will be no ill-feeling on Andreas' part; he admits he knows nothing about sailing beyond the Pillars of Hercules. He will accept you. He will sail her, but if you think you can make her go faster, tell him, and he will do it.'

'We hope,' Hasseler said, suddenly, his eyes on Stallard, 'hey, Mr Stallard?'

Without replying, Stallard gazed back into the eyes of the pale and lazy merchant banker. Hasseler's eyes were the colour of dirty ice, and Stallard now found that, for some reason, he did not like the man.

Unsettled by the intransigence of the other man's eyes, Hasseler asked, 'Do you think you can do it?'

Stallard said, 'If she can sail on Friday, and if the weather isn't too abominable, I can get her there within a month.'

'I want you to do better than that, Victor,' Bazarki said. 'I need to have her there a week before the ceremony. There are going to be many distinguished guests in Jarma for this ceremony. I'm chartering aircraft to bring parties from New York, London, and Paris. At night there is to be a great banquet and the sky will be lit by the most fantastic display of pyrotechnics you've ever seen. There will also be a show, the best performers available will be there for that one night, from Beirut and from Europe. The most important of the visitors will be my guests on the yacht, and I want her there in plenty of time for the caterers and —the window-dressers, you understand.'

Stallard scowled. 'I can't guarantee arrival within three weeks, Jamil.'

'Why not? She has the speed.'

'When the Germans say she'll do forty,' Stallard explained, 'they mean on a millpond, with a following wind. But in any kind of a sea, that sort of speed would just break her up.'

'Try, can you?' Bazarki asked.

'I'll get her there as fast I can,' Stallard promised.

'Presumably you'll have to make a couple of bunkering stops,' Hasseler said to Stallard.

'Presumably,' Stallard nodded, watching the pale, red-lipped man.

'I was just thinking,' Hasseler went on. 'My wife has to be there for this causeway ceremony. Her consultancy represents the State of Jarma diplomatically in London, among other things. And she could use a break, especially after this business of last night.'

29

'What happened last night?' Stallard asked.

Hasseler looked up. 'Haven't you read a paper today? Some journalist fellow called on us. We chucked him out, and shortly after he was murdered.'

Stallard raised his eyebrows.

'That,' Hasseler said, 'on top of all this other business with Sigrid disappearing—well, she needs to get away from it all, and I think a cruise would do her the world of good.'

'Forty knots in an Atlantic gale, Mr Hasseler,' Stallard said, 'is no cruise.'

'Still, it would take her mind off other things,' Hasseler said. 'I was wondering if you could pick her up at your first bunkering port some time next week.'

'It's all right with me,' Stallard said, 'if it's all right with Jamil.'

'Why not?' Bazarki said. 'If you think it would do her good, Conrad, by all means.'

'Thank you,' Hasseler said, without expression, and his slate-grey eyes moved to Stallard. 'I'll tie up the details with you later, by radio.'

Bazarki looked at Stallard too, but he smiled. 'Well, Victor, you are booked on a Lufthansa flight to Fuhlsbuttel, leaving Heathrow in'—he consulted his watch—'two hours' time. Your ticket is with the reception desk downstairs. In the meantime, would you like something stronger than coffee?'

'I'd like to make a phone call,' Stallard said.

'Certainly. Use the phone in the bedroom, if you would prefer it.'

'Thank you.' Stallard went into the bedroom.

As he lifted the receiver, he fancied he heard something —the word, 'No!' whispered urgently, from the ear-piece of the phone. It was so faint and quick that he could have been mistaken, but he was still frowning when the switchboard answered him. He asked for the number of Godwin's flat, then put the receiver down on the bed and walked

on the thick-pile carpet to the door, which he opened
silently.

In the lounge, Hasseler was standing by the phone-table,
the receiver to his ear.

'You've got her number,' Stallard said to him coldly
and with a certain malice, 'but *don't* put it in your little
black book.'

His pale face colouring softly pink, Hasseler began to
put the receiver down.

'Don't hang up,' Stallard said, 'I might as well take it
there as you're going to listen in anyway.' He went back
into the bedroom and hung up the extension. He heard
Bazarki admonishing Hasseler.

'That was stupid, Conrad!'

'I like to know as much as possible about people who
are being involved in my affairs,' Hasseler said, with pique.

Stallard took up the receiver from the phone-table in
the lounge. In Godwin's flat, the phone rang and rang.
There was a cigarette box on the table and he helped himself to one of its contents. The switchboard operator cut
in on the ringing. 'There's no reply at that number, sir.
Shall I try it again?'

'No. Get the *Daily World* for me.'

At that, Hasseler looked round sharply, first at Stallard,
then Bazarki.

The newspaper switchboard answered, Stallard asked for
the news-editor, and when that phone was answered he
asked for Cynthia Godwin.

A man's voice said, 'I'm sorry, she hasn't been in today.
She had a bit of a shock last night, you may find her at her
flat.'

'What shock?' Stallard asked, concerned.

'A colleague of ours was killed last night. A very unpleasant business. Who is this speaking, by the way?'

'Victor Stallard,' Stallard said.

'Ah, Mr Stallard. I've heard a lot about you.'

'She's not at her flat, I've tried there. She's probably

left town. Anyway, when you see her, tell her I rang, will you? And I'll be in touch.'

'Yes, sure.'

He hung up and looked at his watch. He said to Jamil Bazarki, 'I'd better go.'

'Thank you again, Victor, for coming so promptly. And I apologise for the'—he looked at Hasseler—'embarrassment.'

Stallard smiled as he shook hands with the Arab. 'I'll see you in Jarma.' Then he looked across at Hasseler. The pale man stood with his back to the room, one hand in his trouser pocket.

Stallard said, 'Mr Hasseler,' then turned and left.

As he was going out the door, he heard Hasseler say, in a voice that was surprisingly resonant, sonorous, and solemn:

'Mr Stallard.'

3

Godwin had heard of Mrs Black. If you worked in Fleet Street, either at the working-class end, or at the Law Courts end, or even in the middle, you could not help but have heard of Mrs Black. Godwin had even met people who claimed that the lady actually existed; but for the majority she was as the Flying Dutchman to a sailor—a myth.

Yesterday, for Godwin, and for Tod Spencer, the myth had been exploded. Spencer had been working on the Sigrid Hasseler story, and yesterday the girl had been missing for eight or nine days and the story was getting cold. Spencer had been looking for a new angle, a fresh development; but there was none. Then Mrs Black, or a woman calling herself that, had phoned the *Daily World* and asked to speak to him. She had explained that it was about the Sigrid Hasseler story, but she would only speak to Tod Spencer about it; no one else. Tod Spencer had gone off to meet Mrs Black last night, and early the next morning he was found dead in his flat.

There was a club in Mayfair called Mrs Black's; but it was universally assumed that that was just to drag down the tourists. It was universally assumed wrongly, however, because no tourist ever got inside Mrs Black's. There, the clientele was exclusive and very discreet.

The entrance was in an alley off South Audley Street. There was no illuminated sign outside, just a snooty bronze plaque on a great, oak door, engraved 'Mrs Black's Club. Members Only'. To open that door could cost you anything up to £10,000 a year.

On the other side of the door was a liveried commissionaire, a karate First Dan, who, if you had come by your key irregularly or were out of benefit financially, would not let you in. If you proved difficult, there were four more characters, just as expert as he was but in various other forms of combat, upon whom he could rely for assistance.

Beyond the commissionaire stage, you would meet one of the most fantastic half-naked women you had ever met, or ever would meet, and she was the receptionist, and beyond her, having paid your money, you took your chances with some of the most fantastic *stark* naked women in the universe. That is the sort of establishment Mrs Black operated, and that was where Tod Spencer had gone, the night he was murdered.

Whatever happened, Godwin reasoned, she ought at least to warn Mrs Black that the killers of Tod Spencer were now looking for her. The phone number of the club was ex-directory, but Godwin had ways of finding out ex-directory phone numbers. When she had it, she dialled it.

The phone was answered by a crisp, official, secretarial type of bird, saying noncommittally: 'Marion Douglas speaking.'

33

Godwin said, 'My name is Cynthia Godwin. I'm a friend of the late Tod Spencer. I want to talk to Mrs Black, urgently.'

'Hold the line, please.'

She held the line long enough to smoke half a cigarette and finish her current cup of coffee. Then another woman's voice came on, not crisp and cultured this time, but faintly north country.

'Miss Godwin?'

'Are you Mrs Black?' Godwin asked.

'Yes.'

'I feel I ought to advise you, the men who killed Tod Spencer visited me this morning. They were looking for you.'

For a time there was silence on the line. Then the woman said, 'You are Cynthia Godwin of the *Daily World*?'

'Of course I am,' Godwin said.

'And some men visited you. How do you know they were the men who killed Tod Spencer?'

'One of them told me. And he showed me the weapon he used, and he said he was going to kill me too, unless I told him about Tod visiting you last night.'

'And did you tell him?'

'No.'

'Then why aren't you dead?'

'I've got till five o'clock this afternoon.'

'Have you been in touch with the police?'

'No,' Godwin said.

'Why not?'

'I don't need them yet.'

'But you'll need them around five o'clock this afternoon.'

'If nothing—turns up,' Godwin said, hesitantly, 'I suppose I will.'

'What are you going to do in the meantime?'

'I don't really know.'

There was another long silence on the wire, before Mrs

Black said, 'Do you know the name of the man, or the men, who called on you this morning?'

'The boss's name was Davies. Colonel John Davies.'

Again there was a long silence, of which Godwin took advantage to light another cigarette.

Then Mrs Black said, 'Get into a taxi and come over here.'

'But they'll follow me.'

'Let them.'

'But you don't understand, Mrs Black, these men are not ordinary Soho yobbos ...'

'I know what they are, Miss Godwin. Do as I say. And under no circumstances involve the police. I'll expect you within the half-hour.' There was a click and then the rapid purr of the dead line.

And after a moment of conjecture, Godwin also hung up.

The doorbell rang and she jumped a full six inches off the seat. She stared at the door. She had not even bothered to lock it since her callers had left.

She moistened her lips and called, 'Who's there?'

'Mrs McAllister, ma'am,' came the reply.

'Oh,' Godwin breathed. The cleaning woman. The carpet by the settee was stained with vomit where Godwin had fallen after being punched in the chest. Her dress was in shreds on the floor there and she was still in briefs and bra. There was a general aftermath-of-disaster air about the place. She stood and looked at her face in the wall-mirror above the phone. Her upper lip was swollen and colouring darkly, and her hair looked as if she'd spent a week in a wind-tunnel.

She called through the closed door, 'Come back later, Mrs Mac. It's not convenient now.'

'Oh,' said Mrs McAllister, then, 'oh awright then.'

Off she'll go, Godwin imagined, believing I've got a boyo in here and we're on the short-strokes.

There was nothing else for it now but to do as Mrs Black

had instructed. She was, of course, mightily thankful for the invitation, but for other reasons than the obvious. She was in fact almost as anxious to meet Mrs Black as Colonel Davies seemed to be.

She rang for a taxi, then got dressed in a black trouser suit, a wide-brimmed black hat with a white silk scarf and dark, wraparound sun-glasses. Then she went downstairs and got into the taxi.

Travelling across London, she watched through the back window. Yes, she was followed. A nondescript, pale green Ford Cortina, but doctored. She could tell it had been doctored, even from the front, because it was so low slung and because of the fat tyres on the wide-rim wheels that it wore. There was just the driver in it, and from the width of his shoulders she reckoned it was the blond one whom she had hit in the face with the whisky.

In thick traffic at Knightsbridge, she thought for a moment she had lost him; but at Hyde Park Corner he was back again; about three cars behind her, and he kept that distance up Park Lane and on into the Edgware Road. When, at length, her cab turned off South Audley Street into the alley, the Cortina did not follow. He was too clever for that, he knew the alley was a dead-end.

The cab-driver grinned at her, showing a set of National Health teeth with bright orange gums, and said, 'What about an invite, love?'

She looked at the plaque on the door and suddenly realised that the driver had taken her for one of Mrs Black's resident ladies. But she was in no mood for badinage and she just paid her fare and said nothing. She rang the doorbell of this most majestic of all houses of ill-fame, and a metallic male voice asked her, via a speaker set in the doorframe: 'Who is it, please?'

She spoke her name into the speaker. There was an electronic click and the great door opened, seemingly of its own accord, on silent hinges. She stepped into a hall that stank of camphor-wood and rosewater, onto a marble floor.

36

Against one wall, surrounded by great-leaved foliage, a beautiful, white marble lady named Chloe' offered her all for inspection.

A man in a grey sweater and cord jeans greeted her. He was bald and middle-aged, but extremely fit looking and muscular. He took her to one of those antique elevators, like a gilded cage for an ostrich, which are operated by the user heaving mightily on a rope inside the vehicle, and they went up four floors. When the lift stopped, the bald man spoke into a copper-meshed opening in the wall: 'Miss Godwin, ma'am.'

There was no reply, but the latch on the gate of the elevator cage sprang open, released remotely from outside. Then a great steel door slid aside, to admit Godwin to the domain of Mrs Black.

The floor of the lobby here was of polished wood blocks. An ornate and somewhat archaic chandelier hung from the ceiling and on one wall a pair of armour gauntlets were clasped across the blade of a great Crusader sword. On either side of this arrangement was a portrait, one of John F. Kennedy, the other of Pope John the 23rd. On another wall was a flight of ceramic geese, and in the wall facing Godwin as she emerged from the lift was a broad, arched opening giving into the living-room. In this opening stood the fabled Mrs Black.

She presented an attractive though unremarkable figure. She was of medium height and in her thirties. She wore a homely, ankle-length dressing gown, and no make-up. Her hair was naturally blonde, tied back in a pony-tail. Her neck was long, and the bone formation of her face was very good, the cheekbones high and the nose long, classical Greek except for a small irregularity which, in fact, added character. The lips were full and soft and powder pink and, but for the width of her mouth, could have been doll-like; the jaw-line was softly rounded, an utterly female jaw. Her eyes were beautiful, the lashes like finely barbed wire, the eyes blue and their gaze disarmingly direct. They were gazing at Godwin's upper lip.

'Run into a door?' Mrs Black asked, and then she smiled. Her smile was almost motherly, and Godwin felt like a little boy coming home with his trousers torn. 'Come in,' Mrs Black said.

The living-room was enormous and split-level, but the furniture and the general ambience were even more seaside boarding-house than the entrance hall had been. There was even a maid-servant in the livery of seaside boarding-house maid-servants, only this one was a Negress. She wore a black dress with the obligatory frilled white apron and cap. Tea and Danish pastries were ready on a trolley.

'Take your hat off,' Mrs Black said. 'And your glasses.'

Godwin did as requested, and the woman studied her for a moment and then nodded. 'Yes, you're Cynthia Godwin.'

'How do you know?'

'I've seen your picture in the *Daily World*.'

Godwin said, 'It's nice to know somebody buys it.'

'I buy it because of Tod Spencer,' Mrs Black said. 'Tea?'

'Yes, please.'

'Pastry?'

Suddenly Godwin was ravenously hungry, but not for pastries. 'Not really,' she said.

'Would you like anything else?'

'Well,' Godwin hesitated, then plunged in, 'to be brutally frank with you, I'd like bacon and eggs.'

At that, Mrs Black laughed and looked at the maid-servant. She said, 'Lavinia.'

Lavinia, too, was grinning at Godwin. She asked, 'How many eggs, madame?'

'Three, please,' Godwin said.

'Coming right up,' the girl said, and departed for the kitchen.

'How can you eat like that and stay skinny?' Mrs Black asked.

'Easy,' Godwin said. 'I just eat once a week.'

38

Unreasonably, she felt secure here. Safe. Colonel Davies was out there, beyond the iron door, and he could not get at her here.

Having poured the tea, Mrs Black sat down in a deep, ragged-cushioned, chintz-covered arm chair. 'Now tell me about it,' she said.

Godwin lit a cigarette and told the story of her morning. The other woman sipped tea and listened, and when the story was told she said: 'You know who Davies is, of course?'

'No,' Godwin said. 'I've no idea.'

'He's the Chief of Police in Jarma. Actually, a highly respected officer of the law. Ex-British Army, ex-Palestine and Kenya police. He's also a friend of the Hasseler family; visits them whenever he's in London.' The blonde woman rose and began, lightly, gracefully, to pace the floor. She moved easily and distantly, like a dancer. In fact the more Godwin observed this most superior of all madams, the more she realised that the woman was beautiful.

'How long had you known Tod Spencer?' Godwin asked her.

'I didn't know him,' Mrs Black said. 'I never met him in my life until last night.' Then she told her story.

'Seventeen years ago,' she said, 'I was seventeen years old. I had a husband. He was called up in the Army. The Korean war was on, and he was shipped out there. He left me eight months pregnant, in digs in Nottingham. I don't know what the hell I lived on. Black tea and cigarettes. I was broke, the landlady was going to kick me out of the digs because I owed about three months' rent. Then I got this telegram, that he was dead. Killed in action, a noble hero of whom we are all justly proud, and we thank you for your kind contribution, madame, goodbye and bugger you.'

She did not look at Godwin while she spoke. She just paced up and down, looking at the floor, remembering. 'For a while I thought about putting a rug across the door, shutting the windows, and turning on the gas. I didn't because of the baby. I felt I ought to have the baby first, give it a chance to live if it wanted to. Then his mother sent me this cutting from the *Daily World*. I lost the cutting years ago, but I can recite it to you. I know it off by heart.'

She looked at Godwin now, full in the face, her own face deadpan, aloof, and began to recite:

' "He was one of those that they brought in this morning, sixteen of them, by helicopter, from Hill Two-Sixty. Sixteen left out of three platoons, and I think if you put these sixteen together you would not get enough spare parts to make one of them whole again. This lad had no legs and half his gut was gone too. His name was Charlie Black and he used to play football for Nottingham Forest.

' "He was full of morphine, but for a while he was coherent and he asked me for a cigarette. I went outside and waded through the soup that was made out of blood, mud, and snow on the parade ground, searching for somebody who had some cigarettes. When I found one I came back with it, but he was dead. He's lying there dead now, with an unlit cigarette between his lips, and there are fifteen more of them here in this tent and it is starting to stink a little..." '

Godwin stared back into the blonde's lovely, soft blue eyes; then Mrs Black turned away. The passage she had just recited had, for her, all the meaning of life in it, all the unfairness, the cowardice, the stupidity, and the brutality of men. 'Tod Spencer wrote that,' she said, slightly hoarse. 'That was my husband, my Charlie, and that little passage of prose from a newspaper changed my life. I stopped feeling sorry for myself, and I got angry. I thought, right, Charlie, my darling, they got you, but the bastards are not going to get me. No, they are not!'

She turned lightly and began pacing again, slowly and easily, up and down, the dressing gown swinging around her long legs. When she spoke again, the passion had died.

'I went straight out and arranged for my baby to be adopted as soon as it was born. When it was born, they took it off me straight away and I never saw it. Then I set

40

about building this little empire you see about you. I became a prostitute, I learned to dance, to strip, to model, I did anything for anybody provided he could pay. Every penny I made I put away, except what I needed to live on and to make myself desirable for the next customer. The baby was born in '53. In '58 I had enough loot to move to London. By then I was almost respectable, I was a top stripper, making five hundred quid a week. By the time I quit, I was making two thousand a week. But when I first came down here, I was living in a flat at Wembley. The woman in the flat upstairs had a baby.'

She poured herself more tea, and while stirring it she looked at Godwin and continued:

'One thing I did in those digs in Nottingham, waiting for the baby to be born, I knitted a little matineé coat. It was just for something to do, to take my mind off my rumbling stomach. It's the only thing I've ever knitted in my life and it took ages. By the time I'd finished it, I knew the shape of every stitch in the damn thing. Then one day, I looked in the pram of this kid upstairs at Wembley, and he was sitting there with this matinée coat on. The one I'd knitted.

'I asked his mother where she'd got it and she said from a jumble sale at the local primary school. I went down to the school. I didn't dream for a moment that I could find my baby; but if I could, I just wanted to see him—or her —I didn't even know what sex it was. I didn't want to talk, or touch; just see, from a safe distance.'

She stopped talking and gazed rather wanly at Godwin. Then she said, 'Of course you know what's coming.'

'No . . .' Godwin shook her head, stupidly.

'It cost me money,' Mrs Black said. 'But I found my baby. She's Sigrid Hasseler.'

'My God!' Godwin whispered. 'Then they are not her parents.'

'Adoptive parents.'

Lavinia came in with Godwin's breakfast, although it was now after 2 p.m.

41

'One of them is sterile,' Mrs Black said. 'Maybe both.' Meaning the Hasselers. 'So they adopted one. Then they found they weren't cut out for kids, so, wisely, they stopped at one.'

'What do you mean?' Godwin asked, shovelling bacon and eggs into her mouth.

'I don't mean they haven't been good to her,' the blonde said. 'She's had everything any child could want. Except love. She just hasn't had any loving.'

Godwin supposed any mother would feel that way about strangers bringing up her child. But she kept quiet about that.

'I suppose,' Mrs Black said, 'over the past twelve years, I've seen Sigrid no more than six times. I can describe each occasion in minute detail, but I'll spare you that. She, of course, knows nothing of me; she still believes the Hasselers are her natural parents. I don't mind. I don't ever intend to disillusion her on that, I don't ever intend to make myself known to her. But I have contacts. Among the Hasselers' domestic staff here in London, and since the girl's been at the Sorbonne, I've established one or two in Paris. I keep them on retainers, and they keep me so well informed that I in fact know more about Sigrid than her so-called parents do.'

She broke off to sip tea and Godwin, without interrupting breakfast, watched her.

'I know so much about Sigrid,' the woman said, 'that when she went missing I actually thought I knew where she was.'

'Where did you think she was?' Godwin asked.

'In Paris.' There was an abstracted look in Mrs Black's gaze, her eyes focussed on nothing. 'It's· possible she is there, but now I'm not so sure. That's why I telephoned Tod Spencer.' She snapped out of her trance and focussed sharply on Godwin. 'You know Virginia Hasseler runs a public relations organisation, one of whose functions is to represent the state of Jarma diplomatically in London.'

Godwin nodded.

'The state of Jarma is run by a man called Jamil Bazarki,' Mrs Black said. 'He isn't the ruler, but he's the power there. The Bazarki family is the richest on the island, and the most enlightened. Because of Mrs Hasseler's connection with Jarma it was inevitable that Bazarki's son should meet Mrs Hasseler's so-called daughter. Well, they met, and they liked each other. The boy seems, from what I can discover of him, to be a thorough gentleman and quite clever; but, of course, he's an Arab, a Jarmani "native" as Mrs Hasseler calls them, and so the Hasselers disapproved of him as a prospect for Sigrid.'

Godwin had finished breakfast and was dabbing egg off her swollen upper lip. The lip now was numb.

Mrs Black said, 'There was a row between the Hasselers and Sigrid, and they ordered her to break it off with the boy, whose name is Showqi. The next thing I knew she had disappeared in France while driving back to college in Paris, and it was all over the newspapers.'

'So it's pretty obvious she's with Showqi,' Godwin said.

'That's what I thought; and if she is with Showqi, I know where they are, but it would be difficult to check. Showqi studied at the Sorbonne himself. I know that during her terms at the Sorbonne, the girl has spent a number of dirty weekends, as they're called, with Showqi at a place in Montmartre. It's a flat above a map shop in the Rue Richard Bramm. I went there once just to look the place over; I've never seen so many maps, the place is stuffed with them. The old girl who owns it calls herself Madame Celeste, but she's as Arab as Allah; one of her sons was killed by the French police during the Algerian trouble; her other two sons are great friends of Showqi's. The Hasselers know nothing about this place; but if Sigrid is with Showqi, that's where they are.'

'Why do you say it's difficult to check?' Godwin asked.

'Do you know Montmartre? Do you know Soho? The police are looking for Showqi, and Sigrid, and when the police are looking for somebody in a district like that, the place just shuts up tight. No information comes out at all.

Even though I pay my Paris contacts well, they're not prepared to risk going up to Montmarte and asking questions about Showqi—anything could happen; they certainly wouldn't find out anything, and they could end up in the Seine with their throats cut.'

Godwin frowned. 'What makes you doubt that Sigrid and the boy are at this place?' she asked.

Mrs Black sipped more tea. Then she said, 'The night before last, my contact at the Hasseler house here in London came to see me. The Hasselers had received a letter that day, posted in Paris. One of the upstairs maids heard them arguing about it, and in the course of the argument, Virginia Hasseler said: "But it says in the letter, if the Bee Sting Deal goes through, we'll never see her again." '

Godwin frowned deeply this time. Again that day, the Bee Sting Deal.

'That scared me,' Mrs Black said, replacing her empty tea cup on the trolley. 'Maybe she wasn't with Showqi after all. Maybe something bad had indeed happened. I wanted to find out what the hell this Bee Sting Deal was all about; I wanted to know what was the sacrifice the Hasselers had to make. I have an instinctive mistrust of the police, Miss Godwin—I'm afraid it comes naturally to anyone following my line of enterprise. But I thought of that man on the *Daily World*, Tod Spencer, who had written that story all those years ago that had changed my life. I wondered if he could find out for me what the Bee Sting Deal was. So, as you know, I called him and asked him to come over here last night. I told him what I've just told you. As far as I know, he went straight from here last night to the Hasselers' home. He was going to ask them, straight out, what was this Bee Sting Deal. Then'—she looked at the carpet—'then, he was dead.'

Godwin said, quietly, 'Funny.'

'What's funny?'

'That that story he wrote, all those years ago, from Korea, about another man's death, should lead like this, to his own.'

44

The other woman said nothing. Godwin turned and looked at her and the blonde's jaw was tight, her head bowed. She was distressed by the death of Tod Spencer; but she was even more distressed by what it implied for Sigrid Hasseler.

'Whatever it is,' Mrs Black said, 'this deal, it's a damn big one, and the Hasselers are in it up to their necks, and if it's that big it might be more important to them than she is.'

'I see what you mean,' Godwin nodded.

At that moment, the phone rang. Lavinia, the maid, answered it, and then said to Mrs Black, 'It's the private eye, ma'am.'

Mrs Black took the phone, and while she was thus otherwise engaged Godwin turned her attention to a cigarette. Lavinia asked her, 'More tea?' and Godwin said, 'Yes, please.' She was beginning to feel the effects of almost thirty-six hours without sleep.

Mrs Black was ten minutes on the phone. When she finished and hung up she turned, and looked rather strangely at Godwin.

'Miss Godwin,' she said, 'do you know a man named Stallard?'

Godwin stared wide-eyed at the other woman. 'Yes,' she said. 'I do. Why?'

'Who is he?'

'Among other things,' Godwin said, 'He's my—my fiancé. But he's in the Persian Gulf right now.'

'He's not, you know,' Mrs Black said. 'He's here, in London.'

'How on earth do you know that?'

'I've got a firm of private detectives following Conrad Hasseler,' Mrs Black said. 'That was their operative on the phone just now. At one o'clock, Hasseler had lunch with Jamil Bazarki in Bazarki's suite at the Dorchester. At two-thirty this man Stallard arrived. He spent about three-quarters of an hour with them, during which time he tried to phone you. My operative has an "in" with the switchboard there. He tried your flat and then the *Daily World*.

45

He left a message for you at the *Daily World*, to say that he'd called and would be in touch. He's just this minute left the Dorchester the same way he came—in a taxi with his luggage.'

'My God,' Godwin whispered. Then her green eyes blazed. 'The bastard! Why didn't he let me know he was coming?'

'From the despatch with which he came and went at the Dorchester, it would seem he's on a bit of a rush job.'

'But where's he gone?'

'He picked up an airline ticket from the reception desk at the Dorchester. It was for a Lufthansa flight leaving London Airport at five o'clock—for Hamburg.'

'Hamburg,' Godwin whispered, deeply puzzled.

Then Mrs Black said, with urgency, almost imploring, 'Miss Godwin, will you go after him—for me?'

'Yes,' Godwin said, without thinking, 'of course I will.'

The blonde looked at her watch. 'If there's a seat on it,' she said, 'you'll make the same plane.' She picked up the phone. 'Marion,' she said, 'there's a Lufthansa flight leaving Heathrow at five for Hamburg. I want a seat on it, I don't care how much it costs. If it's full they'll just have to chuck somebody out, you understand? The seat is for Cynthia Godwin, and I want a helicopter here, on the roof, immediately, to take her to the airport. Got that?'

Godwin stood staring at the other woman, and Mrs Black turned and looked at her; but there was no woman left in this blonde now, she was one hundred per cent fierce, ruthless businessman. 'Where's your passport?' she asked.

'At the *Daily World*,' Godwin said. 'They keep it to keep my visas up to date, in case I have to go anywhere in a hurry.'

'This is one of those times when you have to go somewhere in a hurry,' Mrs Black said. 'Phone them. I'll send somebody for it. You'll have to give him a written authorisation. Now'—she was thinking hard—'money.'

Godwin was on the phone to the *Daily World*.

The other woman moved aside a picture on the wall and

46

opened a wall safe. She took out a wad of tenners and handed it to Godwin. 'That's five hundred,' she said. 'There's no time for traveller's cheques, you'll just have to stick it in your knickers and smuggle it out in cash. Buy whatever you need when you get there.'

Godwin nodded. She gave her instructions about her passport to the office manager at the *Daily World*. As soon as she hung up, the phone rang and Mrs Black took it. She listened, nodded, then said, 'I want a messenger on a motor-cycle, a fast one. He's got to get to Fleet Street and back within half an hour.' Godwin was already penning an authorisation so that the office would surrender her passport to the messenger.

When she put down the phone, Mrs Black said, 'The flight is okay, and the chopper is on its way.'

The messenger was despatched for Fleet Street.

'Let's have a drink,' Mrs Black said.

'I need one,' Godwin said. 'Badly.' She had a sense of having been shifted so fast her heels hadn't touched the deck.

Mrs Black sat down with a Bacardi and Coke and Godwin settled for brandy. With her soft but penetrating blue eyes, the blonde regarded Godwin steadily. 'Stallard will be frank with you, presumably.'

'Yes,' Godwin said. 'He will.'

'He just might know something that would help me. About the Bee Sting Deal, I mean.'

Godwin looked at Mrs Black for a moment. Then she said, 'Do you want me to go to Paris too?'

The other woman said, 'I've already got Tod Spencer's death on my conscience. I don't want yours as well. I just want you to find out what Stallard knows.'

'I'll do that,' Godwin said. 'But I'll go to Paris, too.'

'I don't want you to go to Paris.'

'Whether you want me to or not, Mrs Black, I'll go. If you want me to do it for you, and I find Sigrid there, then nobody else in the world will know; just you, and I'll forget all about it. But if you won't authorise me to go there on your behalf—then you've given me a lead on a pretty good story, and I'll go as a representative of the *Daily World*.'

Sudden anger flared in Mrs Black's eyes. 'No!'

'It's my job, Mrs Black,' Godwin said, simply.

'Look, Miss Godwin,' the woman said, reasonably, 'my contacts in Paris know the city. They live there. If they can't find out whether Showqi and Sigrid are at Madame Celeste's, how do you expect to do it?'

'What do your contacts do for a living?'

The blonde seemed discomfited by the question. She shrugged irritably, as if her contacts' professions had nothing to do with it. 'One is a designer, one is a—a waitress, and another is a professor at the Sorbonne. But they are all highly intelligent people, Miss . . .'

'Highly intelligent they might be,' Godwin cut in, 'but you've set them a task they simply don't know how to do. Any private detective could do it for you, or any newspaper reporter worth his salt.'

'I don't want to involve reporters or detectives, can't you see? If they are there, they must not be disturbed, or frightened in any way. While they're there, obviously they're safe. If they're alarmed, they might leave there, and try to run, and they'd be picked up by the police as soon as they stepped outside the door. And that's the last thing I want. If she's safe with Showqi, I want to leave them alone.'

'I won't alarm them,' Godwin promised. 'They won't even know I've been there.'

'And you will keep it all strictly confidential?'

'Strictly.'

'Promise me.'

'I promise.'

The other woman looked dubiously for a moment at Godwin. Then she said, 'All right.' She handed Godwin a small card on which was written a phone number. 'As soon as you know anything at all, ring me here. This is my private number, you don't come through the switch-

48

board, and you can reverse the charge, from anywhere. Lavinia, let's have another drink.'

The maid took their glasses back to the liquor cabinet.

Looking steadily at Godwin, Mrs Black said, 'Tell me about this man Stallard.'

'He's a sailor,' Godwin said. 'He was a master mariner. He worked for an oil company, on tankers, but he lost his ticket. It was over a woman, about ten, twelve years ago. His first mate's wife; she was sailing with them—she fancied Stallard and he fancied her. The fellow tried to kill Stallard, and in defending himself Stallard killed the mate. He stood trial for manslaughter, but was acquitted on grounds of self-defence. The fellow had attacked him with a meat cleaver in an alley in Port Said. It was in the dark, and Stallard did not know who his assailant was until it was too late. The Board of Trade took his master's ticket off him, anyway.'

'What does he do now?' Mrs Black asked.

Godwin sipped her drink and looked the other woman straight in the eye. 'He's a smuggler,' she said.

'What does he smuggle?'

'Gold,' Godwin said. 'And booze.'

Mrs Black nodded, slowly. Then she asked, 'Is he straight, Miss Godwin?'

Godwin said, 'He's straight, if you are.'

The woman looked up at her, the blue eyes soft now, no longer piercing, the urgency and the worry, for the moment, gone. Softly, she said to Godwin, 'Thanks.'

4

In the taxi on the way to the airport, Stallard began worrying about Godwin. He had bought a paper and read the story of Tod Spencer's demise. Spencer and Godwin had

49

been colleagues, and it occurred to Stallard that Godwin could also have been involved in whatever it was that had got Spencer murdered.

When he reached the airport he tried to phone her again, at various places he knew she haunted in London, but she was at none of them. It was unlike Stallard to worry; but he was worried now. She was, of course, a journalist, a calling she had chosen knowing that it could lead her into unsavoury situations; and in any situation Cynthia Godwin, above all other women, could look after herself. Stallard knew this, but still he worried. She was the daughter of a rich and powerful man, but Stallard also knew that if she was in trouble her father was the last person on earth she would go to for help. All she asked of her father was: 'Do me no favours.'

He had to go to Hamburg. He could not renege on Jamil Bazarki because of an uncomfortable feeling he had about a nutty woman with whom he happened to be in love. He just wished to God he could have contacted her.

Passengers for his flight were called and as he joined the queue at the departure gate, a tall, slender, and, he imagined, beautiful woman walked across the lounge and stood waiting immediately behind him. He only imagined she was beautiful because he could not see her face—she wore a smart black trouser suit, high, thick-heeled, square-toed green shoes and a wide-brimmed green hat that had a black and white striped band. Around her head, she wore a scarf of the same material as the hat-band, tucked under the collar of the jacket, and her eyes were hidden by black, wraparound sun-glasses. But somehow, Stallard knew, she was familiar to him.

He knew the walk, the body, the chin with the prissy, school-marmish, widow's peak. But there was something wrong with her upper lip.

He looked round again at her. It was impossible, but it had to be her. The mouth tightly set, pinching in her dimples, the straight, sharp, slightly tip-tilted nose, lightly freckled, the high, wide cheekbones, and the way she stood

50

which was the way they never taught her to stand at Roedean, with one hip jutting and her arms folded, staring straight back at all the eyes that were staring at her, and she attracted a lot of eyes.

'Cynthia?' Stallard said to her.

She couldn't contain herself. Her mouth widened in a broad grin. He reached out and took the sun-glasses off her face and those deep green eyes, surrounded by stockades of black lash, were laughing at him.

'You bitch,' he whispered, and took her hands in his.

'Come on,' she said. 'We're holding up the traffic.'

The queue was building up behind them.

'Come on where?' he asked. 'Where the hell are you going?'

'To Hamburg,' she said. 'With you.'

On the plane, she told him of the events of her day.

'I don't like it,' he said, scowling.

'What don't you like, darling?'

'After you've been to Paris,' he said, 'what are you going to do then?'

She shrugged. 'I don't know. It depends what happens in Paris. If Showqi and the girl are there, I'll just phone Mrs Black and relieve her apprehensions; if they're not there, perhaps I'll pick up a lead as to where they are.'

'I don't want you to go back to London,' he said. 'Not while this bastard Davies is there, or until I can go with you.'

'Then what do you suggest I do, darling?'

'Come with me on the yacht.'

'But you'll be sailing tomorrow, or the day after.'

'How long will you be in Paris?'

'If I get there tomorrow,' she said, 'I could have it all wrapped up by Sunday.'

'Monday morning,' he said, 'I'll stand to off Santa Cruz de Tenerife. I'll pick you up there.'

'What if I can't make it?'

'I'll give you our radio call-sign. You can call me at sea, any time, by radio telephone. If you don't call me and

51

you don't turn up in Santa Cruz, I'll leave the yacht there and come looking for you.' He looked around at her, concerned. 'And when I find you, you had better have a bloody good story to tell.'

She grinned. 'I will, darling.'

'Godwin,' he sighed, 'I don't know how you do it, but you get yourself into the most goddam situations.'

They landed at Fuhlsbuttel Airport at about 8.30 and took a taxi into Hamburg, to the St Pauli Landungsbrucken. From there they rode in a water-taxi down the Elbe to the Breitenfelder company's wharf where the long, low *Shaheen* sat, serene as a sleeping swan, on the black water. She had been built to be owned by rich men, and as rich men can usually choose their weather, she had never been put out in any kind of a sea, to really earn her living; a pampered boat, sailed by pampered people; but she was undeniably beautiful. She had a hull like a clipper-ship, a long, lancing bowsprit and an overhung transom, designed for speed on millpond waters. How she would react to an Atlantic swell and the push of two 1,000 horse-power diesels was anybody's guess.

Stallard left his bag on the wharf and he and Godwin went up the gang-plank and aboard. The side deck was deserted. He walked along to the stern and peered in. at a window of the deck housing from which a light shone. The room was a lounge with an untended bar in one corner, and its sole occupant was seated at a table, poring over a newspaper. When Stallard knocked on the glass the man looked up, then stood in a state of mild shock, staring at the face in the window.

He was a short, slight Arab, in his twenties, wearing impeccable whites with the insignia of an engineer officer on the epaulettes. He rushed to the lounge room door and flung it open.

'Mr Stallard?' he said, breathlessly; 'yes, sir, I am expecting you, sir, come in, sir.' Then he saw Godwin. 'And Mrs Stallard too, please, to come in, sir.'

As she entered, Godwin smiled at the boy and said, 'I'm not sir. I'm madame.'

'Yes, sir,' the boy said again, wide-eyed with fright, 'you are very welcome indeed, sir, please to come in.'

'Who are you?' Stallard asked him.

'I am Ali Mohamed Makhoza, sir.'

'Jarmani?'

'Yes, Jarmani,' Ali Mohamed said and then grinned, exposing a great keyboard of betel-stained teeth. 'Scottish Jarmani. *Mak*-hoza.'

Stallard grinned back at the boy. Somewhere along the line there is some Scot in all ship's engineers. 'Where's the captain?' Stallard asked him.

'He is ashore, sir.' The boy was suddenly serious again.

'The other officers?'

'They are ashore, sir. I am officer on watch.'

'Is there anyone in the radio-shack? Anyone in the engine-room?'

'There is a man in the engine-room, sir. I am looking after engines too.'

'You knew I was coming tonight?' Stallard asked.

'Oh yes, sir. I am told to expect you.'

To Godwin, Stallard said, 'This is Andreas' way of expressing his disapproval.'

For a moment, while he lit a cheroot, he studied Ali Mohamed Makhoza, who shifted uncomfortably under the scrutiny. This, Stallard thought, is going to be one bloody awful trip.

To Ali Mohamed, Godwin said, 'We know about the radio-shack and the engine-room. Tell me, is there anyone in the galley?'

'Oh yes, madame,' the boy said, then laughed. 'I call you sir, I apologise, you are madame, of course. It is the trousers that confuse me. You are hungry? You want food? I will bring a steward.'

'My luggage is down on the wharf,' Stallard said.

'Yes, sir, it will be brought aboard immediately.'

The engineer disappeared through a door to one side of the bar.

In due course, Stallard and Godwin were served with food and drink there in the lounge and Stallard questioned Ali Mohamed about the yacht's condition. The Breitenfelder company had carried out sea-trials, and their engineers' reports were available. Stores and water were in, and all she needed now was bunkering and customs and health clearances, and she was ready for sea.

Then, his meal consumed, Stallard sat back and said to Ali, 'Miss Godwin and I will go to bed now. When the captain comes aboard, tell him I'll see him and the other officers in this room at ten o'clock in the morning. Miss Godwin and I will have breakfast in the cabin at eight-thirty.'

'Okay, sir,' said Ali Mohamed.

Godwin was looking, expectantly, at Stallard.

'Well?' he said to her.

'Let's go to bed then,' she said, softly.

In the morning, before she left for Paris, Godwin put through a call to Mrs Black in London. Stallard saw her off in a cab from the landing stage and then, not relishing the prospect, went back to the yacht to confront Andreas the Greek.

5

A long, slow, flesh-pink dawn was rising out of the Sahara, turning the black water of the bay of Santa Cruz de Tenerife to limpid green. Stallard stood on the bridge of *Shaheen* and watched the tender coming out from behind the long breakwater enclosing the harbour. Beyond and above the breakwater, across the harbour, stood the white buildings of the Nautical Club and the jumble of roofs and windows which was the town, dominated from this aspect by the Palace and the Spanish Civil War monument, all of it clustered like a child's discarded toys about the foot of the cliffs. The cliffs rose steeply behind the city, away to La Laguna, inland, and the whole of this silent, beautiful land- and seascape seemed cowed beneath the splendour of El Teide, the Peak of Tenerife, rising through low-lying carpets of mist away to the south-west, and hanging in the sky like a phantom mountain. Stallard could not remember how many times, nor from the decks of how many ships, he had seen the Peak, but he was now, as ever before, awed by it.

He was smoking a black cheroot and gripping a mug of black coffee. On the run down they had encountered a small swell across Biscay, and he had tried pushing the yacht through it at full ahead. She had gone through the big, green seas like a destroyer, but she was not built for it, like a destroyer is, and he knew that too much of it would break her up. But she had kept going, kept her keel in the water, and that was the main thing. Her crew had not come through with such flying colours. Andreas had been sick, and his men on the bridge had been treated to the spectacle of their captain hanging over the wing delivering up his insides to the Atlantic. The more that the big Greek saw of Stallard, the more he hated him; but that, in the Bay, had only been a small swell, and Stallard wondered how the yacht and her company were going to perform further south, where they stood to meet some real weather.

The tender came alongside and he quit the bridge and went down to the side deck where a gang-ladder had been lowered. Godwin came up and put her arms round him and kissed him fervently, and he held her tightly, almost in wonder, because when they parted in Hamburg he had been uncertain as to whether he was ever going to see her alive again. His relief was tempered, however, by what she had brought with her. As Mrs Black had surmised, Showqi Bazarki and Sigrid Hasseler had indeed been hiding out at Madame Celeste's in Paris. Showqi had decided that

Europe was getting too hot for him, so Godwin had generously offered to help him get out, so here they were. After all, the yacht did belong to the boy's father, so Stallard could hardly refuse him and the girl permission to join.

Stallard already knew Showqi—they had met at some function or other in the Gulf a year or two ago. He had not met Miss Hasseler before, however. She was a more fully developed female than Godwin, despite that she was just a little more than two-thirds of Godwin's age. Some of it was puppy-fat, but most of it was woman, and all of it was upholstered in silk-smooth, olive-tanned skin. There was a pout about her full lips, but she had straight, direct eyes, with a sense of humour in them, and she had short, straight, slate-coloured hair; it had been cut and dyed that way since her 'disappearance' in France. She wore very short dungaree shorts and a sleeveless black tee-shirt so tight it might have been painted on across the breasts which were otherwise, quite obviously, unhampered.

Showqi was more formally dressed, in a yellow suit and a navy blue silk shirt. His hair was long, but well barbered, and he had a disarmingly natural manner for which Stallard felt disposed to forgive him for being so young.

Later, as the *Shaheen* drove south, Stallard joined the new arrivals for breakfast and heard their story.

'How did you get out of France?' he asked the boy.

Showqi smiled. 'Madame Celeste, besides forging antique and very valuable maps, also forges passports.'

Godwin said, 'We flew to Madrid yesterday afternoon. That's where I called you from . . .' He had taken a radio-telephone call from her yesterday off the Portuguese coast. 'We flew down to Santa Cruz last night.'

'It all started,' Sigrid Hasseler said, 'when Showqi got a bee in his ear about this Bee Sting Deal thing.'

'I learned about it from a tape recording that came into my possession,' Showqi said. 'If you send the steward for a tape player you can hear it. Anyway, I reasoned that this deal was no good for Jarma, and I reasoned that Conrad Hasseler was behind it, because Hasseler has had dealings

56

with men in London from the Russian Embassy. Sigrid told me that. Anyway, Sigrid agreed to co-operate; she was going back to the Sorbonne, and I arranged to meet her as soon as she got to France. I wanted it to look as if she'd been kidnapped.'

'So you wrote the letter to Hasseler,' Stallard said.

'Yes,' Showqi said.

'What I can't understand,' Sigrid Hasseler said, 'is how Miss Godwin found us in Paris.'

'You should never ask a reporter for the source of his information,' Godwin said, quietly.

'And what do you think the Bee Sting Deal involves?' Stallard asked Showqi.

The boy shrugged. 'It's something to do with the Jarma Causeway. There is a great deal of bad feeling in Jarma over this causeway, you know? I have always opposed it, and my father knows this. I and many other Jarmanis do not want it. Oh yes, we want what it will bring, in the way of prosperity and social services, but not what it will mean to us as a people, an independent state—we are Arabs, we do not want to be governed by Persians. The Iranian take-over of Jarma will deprive us not only of our statehood, but of our racial integrity. There are those of us who prefer to remain ignorant and unblest, and to die young but as free, Arab Jarmanis, than to be educated, and kept, and prosperous, as tax-paying Persians. Those of us who are of this persuasion, we call ourselves the Jarma National Front. Yes, we are a political party, a secret one of course as all political parties are banned in Jarma. It is our dearest wish to see the Jarma Causeway blown sky-high. But we are not behind the Bee Sting Deal.'

A tape recorder was ferried in and set up and Showqi put his reel of tape on it, threaded it, and switched it on. The tape started to play. There was a great deal of fuzzing and background crackle, but the voice came over clearly enough. It was male, soft-spoken, and unmistakably American.

'My name is Charles Schreiber. I was an engineer employed on the construction of the Jarma Causeway. I worked on the causeway in Jarma and in Iran throughout the entire four years of the job. Now that it's finished, I would like to say a few words about it, for the benefit of anybody who may be interested. I won't read out all the figures and statistics, but I have them on paper, and they're in a safe deposit box in a bank in New York City. The Jarma Causeway job was costed at 120 million dollars. In fact, as I work it out, it cost just under 40 million dollars. This fantastic saving was effected in this way: the whole job was scaled down from the original plan by a factor of seventeen per cent—any order higher than this, they computed, and the difference between the finished job and the original plan would have been visibly noticeable. Whereas the plan called for a pylon every one hundred and ninety-eight metres, the pylons were actually spaced at intervals of three hundred and three metres, thus eliminating sixty-two sets of pylons completely. Throughout, cheap grade materials were used, and only at points of maximum stress was concrete reinforced. Very few welds were made by qualified welders, most of the welding was done by local Arabs who had about three weeks' instruction in the art before being put to work. No welds were ever tested, or examined by X-ray. I estimate that, if the causeway is used sparingly and by light traffic only, and is not hit by any strong winds or sea turbulence, it might stand up for about twelve months, but serious deterioration will have become noticeable well within that period, in the form of cracks in the roadway. I am not certain as to what was actually done underwater, but I suspect that none of the pylons is bedded in rock, but only in blast holes in the coral on the sea-bed. In making this statement I am in breach of my contract with the Greenhalgh company, the Jarma Causeway Company, and the Iranian and Jarmani Governments. But somebody, somewhere, is making an awful lot of money out of this causeway, which is probably going to kill some people when it collapses.' There was a crackling pause while the tape ran on. Then the American said, 'And it will collapse.'

The voice stopped. The tape wheeled on, a fuzzing sound coming from the speaker.

'Is that it?' Stallard asked.

Showqi Bazarki shook his head, gesturing for silence, and looked back at the tape player.

The American started again: 'In gathering the actual figures and engineering drawings and computer data which are in my possession and which substantiate the statements I have just made, I had to commit the crime of—I believe it's called breaking and entering. I broke into and entered the house of Jamil Bazarki in Jarma, and managed to gain access to a room that was, at that time, being used as an office by Conrad Hasseler, and another man, whom I believe is a Russian. His name is Severin, but I don't know what his function is. He hasn't been out there long. But among the papers I examined in that office was a sheet of the Greenhalgh company's memorandum paper, a memo addressed to Conrad Hasseler. It said, simply, "Bee Sting is a deal". I don't know who the memo came from to Hasseler, I don't know what it meant. But I've been doing some figuring. I figure when that causeway collapses, somebody, like Conrad Hasseler, is going to have a lot of explaining to do. I figure that the only way he can avoid that eventuality is by destroying the causeway himself, before nature does the job for him. It would be a simple enough job, the means are already there, the explosive charges are already set. All that is needed is a reason, an excuse, an explanation of why the charges were detonated. It could be made to look like an accident, and I think that maybe that's what the Russian is there for. Maybe he's a saboteur, a demolition expert. Of course, this is all conjecture. I don't possess a single solitary fact, hard or soft, concerning the Bee Sting Deal. This is just how I've figured it out.'

Then there was silence on the tape. Showqi Bazarki stood up and switched the machine off. 'From the quality of this tape,' the boy said, 'I would say that it's a copy, made from a master tape. I don't know how many copies there are of this tape, or what he did with them. This one he posted to me, at my flat in London. Very shortly after —it must have been less than twelve hours after he posted this tape to me, he was murdered, in New York.'

Stallard scowled. 'By Colonel Davies?'

'If it was Davies,' Showqi said, 'he used a different technique to the one he used on Mr Spencer in London. This man, Schreiber, was shot through the head with a 7.65 millimetre calibre bullet.'

'We know what he did with one of the tapes, at least,' Godwin said. 'He sent it to a New York newspaper.'

'And what are they doing with it?' Stallard asked.

'As far as I can discover,' the boy said, 'nothing.'

Stallard asked, 'What did he mean when he said it would be simple to blow up the causeway, as the charges had already been set? What does that mean?'

'By agreement between the two governments,' Showqi explained, 'of Jarma and Iran, water-tight compartments were built into the bases of the pylons of the Jarma Causeway. In each of these compartments is housed two hundred pounds of trinitrotoluene, and the charges can be detonated in the event of certain circumstances arising— for example, the invasion of Persia by Russia, or the rise of a power in either country unacceptable to the government of the other. Under such circumstances, the causeway would be demolished.'

Stallard was smoking a cigarette and drinking black coffee. Godwin said to him, 'What do you make of it?'

'That sounds like the Bee Sting Deal to me,' Stallard said. 'The government of Jarma had to put up a third of the cost of the causeway and the Persians put up the rest. Right?'

'Right,' Showqi said.

'The Jarma contribution, therefore, was forty million dollars, which was supplied by the Greenhalgh Banking Company—Corporation—or whatever, of which Hasseler is president. The loan was negotiated on behalf of Jarma by Mrs Hasseler's PR outfit in Geneva. The main contractors on the job were the Jarma Causeway Company, presumably a company formed by Hasseler for the specific purpose of building the Jarma Causeway.'

Showqi nodded.

Stallard went on, 'The Jarma Government put up forty million, the Iranian Government put up eighty million, and the cost of the job was forty million. So somebody somewhere, like Conrad Hasseler for instance, is making a cool eighty million dollars clear profit.'

'Yes,' Showqi said, 'and for that reason, I have assumed that Hasseler is behind the Bee Sting Deal. But that is not the deal, it may be part of it, but it is not all of it. The Bee Sting Deal is something far bigger. There is something else going on in Jarma, I don't know what it is and my father refuses to listen to me, he is so wrapped up in his grand opening ceremony. There is that Russian who was mentioned on the tape, Severin. I have seen this man in Jarma. There is a strange ship in the harbour there, Liberian registration but God knows who she is on lease or charter to; she brought two big barges with her and they have been taken up into the Cut. You know the Cut, in Jarma Harbour? On the south side, a deep, narrow canyon, like a little fiord. It goes back about half a mile. You can't see down into it from above, because the cliffs overhang so much. You can't see up into it, because it bends, and you can't go up into it on the water because the entrance is now being guarded by an armed boat. But whatever is going on up there in the Cut, I feel if we knew what it was we would know what the Bee Sting Deal is.'

Lighting another cigarette, Stallard looked at the boy. 'So you decided to try to scare Conrad Hasseler by using Sigrid.'

'What else could I do? Okay, so maybe it was a crazy idea and I know he saw through it as soon as I wrote that crazy letter from Paris. But you've heard this tape. I've had it transcribed, I've sent copies to my organisation in

Jarma, the National Front. They have had copies of it delivered to the Government of Iran in Teheran; they have made representations to the Jarmani Government. I have had British M.P.s lobbied in the House of Commons with this information. Charles Schreiber sent a copy of the tape to a New York paper. But nobody, none of them, is taking the slightest bit of notice of it, nobody is doing anything about it. I feel I am punching a jelly, you know? And I will go on punching it and having no effect on it until I drop dead of frustration and exhaustion. I was desperate when I used Sigrid against her father.'

Stallard nodded sympathetically. 'So what are your plans now?'

The boy shrugged. 'It seems I'm just beating my head against a brick wall in Europe. You're going back to Jarma, I might as well go with you.'

'You don't agree with the American's assessment of this Russian, Severin, in Jarma, that he's a demolition expert, a saboteur?'

'The American didn't know about this business in the Cut. I feel more inclined to believe that the Russian is somehow connected with that. Whatever it is.'

'Then how is Conrad Hasseler connected with it?'

'Through the Bee Sting Deal,' Showqi said, and then he smiled rather wanly.

'So we're back to square one,' Godwin said, flatly.

Shaheen was now going flat out across the Gulf of Guinea on a course for Luanda, in Angola. Stallard intended to refuel her there, and thereafter, according to his calculations and provided that no really foul weather was encountered, she would make it to Jarma without having to bunker again.

In bringing Godwin, Showqi Bazarki, and Sigrid Hasseler aboard, he had not considered the consequences; now he was forced to. He knew that every move he made was being radioed straight to Jamil Bazarki in London, by Andreas. Bazarki would therefore know, whether Stallard wanted him to or not, that the yacht was going into Luanda,

62

and so Conrad Hasseler would know it, because Hasseler was Bazarki's trusted friend, and Hasseler wanted his wife to join the yacht at the bunkering port. Therefore, it was highly likely that Colonel Davies would be waiting in Luanda.

There was nothing much Stallard could do about it now. He did not intend to go alongside; he would anchor in the roads and refuel from a barge and nobody would even have to go ashore. That would not make it impossible for Davies to get at them, but certainly more difficult.

That is how he planned it, but that, in the event, was not how it turned out. In the late afternoon of the day before *Shaheen* was due at Luanda, a message was received from Jamil Bazarki. Smiling rather enigmatically, Andreas delivered it personally to Stallard, who was taking a sundowner on the after deck. It has to be good, Stallard thought ruefully, seeing Andreas' expression. He set his drink down on the trolley and read the pencil-scrawled message by the flame red light of the sunset.

Telephone call person to person Bazarki Stallard. Booked 1100 Weds 24th. Stallard to receive call at hotel Sao Paolo de Luanda. Signed Bazarki.

As the implications of this message dawned on him, Stallard smiled grimly at Andreas, and from the smirk on the fat Greek's face, Stallard judged that the implications of the message were dawning on him too. 'Thank you,' Stallard said.

'My pleasure, Captain,' Andreas said, 'see you at dinner.' Then he left, waddling away along the site-deck.

The message, of course, meant that he would have to go ashore. He leaned against the rail for a while, thinking. Before him on the deck were the two women. Sigrid Hasseler had been lying there in the sun on a floral-pattern camp-bed throughout the afternoon, and a deep, rich suntan covered her long, full, nearly naked body under a glistening patina of oil. Godwin was asleep in a swing-seat under a canopy, out of the sun. A flat-crowned, broad-brimmed straw hat covered her face, and she wore just a little more than Sigrid, a navy blue bikini. By comparison with the girl's, Godwin's body was narrow, somehow younger looking, and stark white, like a greyhound beside a lioness.

Walking across to the swing, he woke Godwin and indicated that she should follow him down to the stern rail. He leaned on the rail and looked down at the yacht's wake which was pink, like froth on a strawberry milk-shake, in the glow of the great red fire in the west. Stallard showed Godwin the message from London and explained what it meant.

'Then don't go ashore,' she told him.

'I can't buck it,' he said. 'It's an order from the owner.'

'Why can't you buck it and sail on?'

'Because of Andreas. If I don't comply with the order, he can enforce it.'

'Give me a cigarette,' she said, and shivered suddenly.

He lit her a cigarette, and then she said, 'Davies will be waiting for you. By now he'll know I'm with you—Andreas will have informed London—and Davies must get to me to get to Mrs Black.'

'Yes,' Stallard said softly. 'As I said once before, you do get involved in some ludicrous situations, darling.'

'I didn't think you'd be dragged into it like this, Vic.'

Ruefully, he grinned at her. 'Like hell you didn't,' he said to her.

The coral reef that encloses the port of Luanda looked like a milk-slick in the limpid green water of the Bay of Bongo as the *Shaheen* dropped her anchor just inside it the next morning and Stallard leaned on the rail and gazed out across the sea to the old town, crouching on a cliff in a nook in the bay. It looked, he thought, more like Portofino, or even Beirut, than an African town, with its terraces of little old houses, mud-yellow and white and pink in the sunshine, and each house with its own, individual roof quaintly tiled and steep rising tier upon tier around the lower flanks of the heavily wooded mountain that climbed into the deep blue sky above and behind them.

Just after 10 a.m., two of the yacht's crew took him in on her tender and he stepped ashore on to a stone pier and was in Africa again, after an absence of about twelve years. The last time had been in Somaliland, on the other side of the great continent, two and a half thousand miles from this place; but the stench of Africa is the same wherever you step ashore, of hot dust and dry dung and the odour of big animals. He went into a small office and had his passport stamped by a sweating Portuguese in a khaki bush shirt who was so busy trying to do a deal with two African women over a basket of pineapples that he did not even look at the passport. Stallard understood a couple of the words that were said because they were Swahili, but the language generally seemed to be a patois of Hottentot and Portuguese. He went out of this office and through the dock area into the narrow, steep, cobbled streets of Luanda, and hailed a taxi.

At about twenty past ten he was sitting in the bar of the Hotel de Sao Paolo de Luanda, drinking iced Portuguese beer. The bar was large and baroque with a marble floor and great, pointed windows, like a cathedral, and a high, arched ceiling from which, on long pipes, fans hung, lethargically rotating. He had not been followed here, and as far as he could see there was nobody waiting here for him, which surprised him somewhat. There were four men at another table who were obviously businessmen, poring over papers and drinking wine and *pastis*, and there was a flamboyantly dressed woman on a stool at the bar who possibly was not a whore, but she looked like one. There were two barmen, both European, and a boy who seemed to serve as waiter, floor-mopper, messenger, and general factotum. Beyond the bar, in the foyer, there was the usual traffic, none of it suspicious. A shoe-shine boy approached Stallard hopefully, but was told to go to hell. I am now such a sitting duck, Stallard thought, that Davies is not even bothering to be here to meet me—he's going to take his time and drop me with a rifle from a respectable distance.

Stallard had drunk three beers in ten minutes when the receptionist came through to tell him his call from London was on the line. She was a tall, elegant girl, of mixed black and white extraction, and she spoke a little French which made her probably one of the very few people in this place with whom he could communicate. He followed her out into the foyer where she indicated a vacant phone booth.

Inside the booth, with the door closed, the heat was incredible. He lifted the receiver and immediately it shone wet with the sweat of his hand. The voice of Jamil Bazarki came to him clearly from London, with only a faint background crackle on the wire.

'Vic, I'm sorry, but I'm going to have to call it off.'

'Call what off?' Stallard asked.

'The yacht, I have to ask you to leave her there, and I'll pay your air fare from there to Bahrain.'

'Are you crazy?'

'No, Vic. Andreas is my old friend. He says if you don't go, he goes, so I have no choice. I must ask you to leave.'

Stallard stood there in the stifling phone box, sweating, silent.

Bazarki said, 'Vic?'

'Yes,' Stallard said, 'all right.'

'I'm sorry, Vic, I am genuinely sorry, but you must understand my position. I have to live with Andreas and his men.'

'Bullshit,' Stallard said, rudely. 'The commission you gave me was to get your yacht into the Gulf in time for your goddam party, and I understood I had to do that at any cost, whether I upset Andreas or blew the boat's gaskets or tore her apart didn't matter so long as I got her there.'

'Well, I've had to revise my thinking. You certainly won't be out of pocket, I assure you. Five thousand dollars will be with the Bank of Angola in your name later today. Also, there will be four air tickets in your name at the head

66

office of South African Airways. They are open tickets, you can go anywhere in the world on them.'

'Four?' Stallard asked.

'Your guests will have to leave the yacht with you. I understand they are Miss Godwin and some others. I only authorised one passenger, Vic, and that was Mrs Hasseler.'

'Do you know who the *some others* are?' Stallard asked.

'I don't want to know. Just get them off my boat.'

'One of them is your son!'

'I don't give a damn if it's the Pope of Rome, Vic, he and his friend leave the yacht with you, and if they don't, Andreas has my authority to call the local police and have you all physically carried ashore. Now goodbye!'

The line clicked, then buzzed. In London, Bazarki had hung up.

Stallard, however, did not hang up. He was sweating profusely and his clothes were wringing wet. His left ear sweated against the ear-piece of the receiver. He stood as if the phone conversation were still continuing because of the possibility that, through the glass-panelled door at his back, he was now being watched. He could not afford now to take a single, avoidable chance. With his right hand he managed to light a cigarette, while this new situation crystallised itself in his mind.

He and Godwin and Showqi Bazarki and Sigrid Hasseler were being set up. They were being stuck on the beach, far from contacts, in a town none of them knew and where none of them even spoke the language. It was like standing bottles on a fence for Davies to take pot-shots at. The money that was going to be in the Bank of Angola 'later today' was merely to keep him hanging around to give Davies plenty of time to take very careful aim.

Rarely in his life before had Stallard felt quite so alone and vulnerable as he did now. But even as these thoughts came to him, his brain was working hard on the problem at hand.

On the wall above the phone ahead of him, cards were pinned advertising the wares and services offered by various commercial enterprises of the town. Two or three of the cards advertised cars for hire. A car, he reckoned, was what he would need, but he had to think more about it. The phone box was suffocating him, and anyway he would have a couple of hours' grace now—Davies would not try anything until he had got the others ashore. Yes, that was it, that was what the money at the bank 'later today' was for—to give Andreas time to get the yacht clear before the killing started. If any or all of her passengers were murdered before the yacht sailed, she would be tied up by the police and held while inquiries were made, and they would not want that. Having worked that out, he felt slightly more secure.

They would not bunker the yacht now, that was for sure. As soon as the disembarkees were off, she would sail. It gave Stallard an hour, maybe two, but if he used that time properly, he might get away with it. He had to move very fast. The airport was out of the question, it meant sitting around, exposed, in waiting halls and departure lounges. He had to bring the others ashore and move them out of this town in one long, continuous, flowing, and bloody rapid motion. And that meant a car.

He hung up the phone and stepped out of the booth into the blessed relief of the comparatively cool hotel foyer. While he attempted to dry off his face with a wet handkerchief, he scanned the faces around him. Still, none of them gave him any cause for alarm. He went to the reception desk and smiled at the nice half-caste girl.

She said, 'Monsieur?'

'I want to hire a car,' he said.

'Yes,' she said, and presented him with a roneoed fool-scap page with the name of a car hire firm at the top, a list of its rules and regulations, and then a list of the cars it could supply. The cars were two in number, a Cadillac Fleetwood sedan with air-conditioning, and a Lincoln Continental convertible.

'I'll have the Cadillac,' Stallard told her.

He handed over his passport and international driving

licence and signed the necessary travellers cheques, also one for an extra two hundred and fifty dollars' worth of cash. He also had to sign a couple of forms which he could not read because they were in Portuguese, which the girl filled in with details from his passport and licence. 'You want the car immediately?' she asked.

'I want it at the dock gates in one hour, with a full tank,' he said.

'*Oui*, monsieur,' she said, then smiled apologetically. 'A full tank will be another twenty-seven dollars.'

He shrugged and started peeling the notes off his roll. 'That seems reasonable,' he said, and smiled back at her.

Having taken his bearings on the taxi ride up, he walked back to the dock, down sloping streets and across little plazas where fat women haggled at barrows piled with fruit and flowers and blue china and cheap toys. Men lounged at tables on café terraces in the sun, drinking beer, brushing away flies. It is like Naples, Stallard thought. You could stand up there where he was and look out across the juxtaposed, cracked and busted plain of round-tiled roofs baking in the sun, across the pale green water of the bay, and almost expect to see Capri on the horizon, but there was nothing out there for three thousand miles, just the wide Atlantic.

On the way down, he passed a sporting goods store which had some rifles chained in a rack standing in the open doorway. He went in and bought an F.N. Supreme, 30.06 calibre, and a hundred rounds. That cost him a hundred and eighty dollars, give or take a dollar. And then, as soon as he found a place that sold them, he bought a rather crude road-map of the country he was in. At the dock, he paid a native boatman to take him out to the *Shaheen*.

As he had suspected, there was no bunker barge tied up alongside her. Godwin greeted him at the top of the gang-ladder. 'What happened?' she asked, anxiously.

Andreas was grinning broadly. For a moment Stallard looked blankly at the Greek, while sweat ran on his body. Then he took Godwin's arm and ushered her along to the stern sun-deck where the other two were. Showqi lounged in a deck-chair in a white canvas hat, swim-shorts, and sandals, and the girl lay face down on the camp-bed wearing her St Tropez rig, just a very brief pair of bikini briefs. Her body glistened, deep rouge, tanned satin.

'Showqi,' Stallard said, sounding almost exhausted, 'we've got to go. Pack your bag. And hers too.' He nodded at Sigrid Hasseler.

The boy looked up at him.

Stallard said, 'We've been ordered off by your father.'

The girl raised herself on her elbows and looked over her shoulder and up at Stallard, through her sun-glasses. Her full breasts hung between her arms on the sweat-damp canvas of the camp-bed.

Stallard told them about his phone conversation with Jamil Bazarki. Upon hearing it, Showqi went a little mad and leapt to his feet. 'But I've got to get to Jarma! It is absolutely imperative!'

'If you shut up and do exactly as I say,' Stallard told him, 'you might make it. Now go and get ready. And don't bring anything that isn't absolutely essential. We've got to travel fast and light.'

Sigrid Hasseler got to her feet and stood with her arms folded across her breasts. 'How do I know what's essential, Mr Stallard?' she asked, 'when I don't know where we're going.'

'Well,' he said, and looked her up and down while he lit a cigarette, slowly, 'start with a shirt, huh?'

She grinned, and then laughed at him, and skipped off across the hot deck planks.

'Blatant bitch!' Godwin whispered, watching Stallard's eyes on the girl.

'Are you ready?' Stallard asked her.

She was wearing a black, sleeveless blouse, black shorts, and leather flipflops. 'As I'll ever be,' she said.

He turned from her and leaned on his elbows on the rail. The F.N. in its canvas case was leaned against the rail beside him.

'Do you want me to pack anything for you?' she asked.

'No,' he said.

'Vic,' she asked him, softly. 'Where are we going?'

He looked out across the bay to the thin, dusty, green edge of vast Africa. 'Darling,' he said, 'I haven't got a clue.'

6

The car was indeed a Cadillac Fleetwood sedan—a twelve-year-old one. It had started out black, but the red dust and the sun of Africa had changed all that. It had those high fins at the back and it lay right down on its aged suspension on cracked, grey, once whitewall tyres. The boy who handed it over to Stallard at the dock gate was, however, obviously very proud of it. It was the flagship of this car-hire firm's fleet.

Stallard slid in behind the wheel and started the engine. Godwin was beside him and the F.N. rifle lay along the seat behind their backsides. Showqi Bazarki and the girl got in the back and Stallard turned the select lever onto Drive and touched the gas pedal and they moved smoothly forward into the dusty, palely blazing street. With the windows shut, the car's air-conditioning blew luxuriously cool. He had memorised his route out of town from the map he had bought.

As he drove, he watched the rear-view mirror constantly, but they were not followed. They drove up through the old town and then along the broad, level avenues of new Luanda. The road was climbing all the time through heavily wooded country, towards a place named on the road signs as Kabanda.

They passed through a broad, sprawling shanty-town suburb that straggled along the verges of the road. It was a place built mainly of corrugated iron, plaited palm fronds

71

and plywood, and occupied by the human rubble which, all over Africa and Asia, is thrown off in the collision between Western culture and the primitive.

Sigrid Hasseler leaned forward and put her hand on Stallard's shoulder.

'Yes?' he asked.

'May I call you Vic?'

'If you want to.'

'Thank you, Vic. Now tell me, would it be an impertinence to ask, where are we going?'

'It wouldn't,' Stallard said. 'No.'

'Then,' the girl said, 'where are we going?'

'I don't know,' Stallard said.

Godwin looked around at the girl and shrugged.

'Then can you tell me why we don't just go to the airport, if there is an airport, and get a plane out of here? To Paris or somewhere, where the environment is a little more salubrious?'

'There's an airport,' Stallard nodded, 'and we could go to it. But I don't think we'd get a plane.'

'You think Colonel Davies would be there?'

'Maybe not in person, but he'd have it covered. And the banks and the airline offices in town, and probably by now, the hotels as well.'

'What you're saying, Vic,' Godwin said, 'is that Jamil Bazarki chucked us off his yacht so that Colonel Davies could have a crack at killing us—"us" including Jamil's own son . . .' She looked around at Showqi in the back seat. 'Do you think your father would have you murdered, Showqi?'

'I have no father,' the boy said. 'Or, to be more precise, my father has no son. When he learned I was a member of the Jarma National Front, he disowned me, disinherited me, and cast me out of his house. Yes, if I looked like impeding the fruition of his great vision for Jarma, he would kill me.'

'Has he heard the tape?' Stallard asked.

'Of course he has heard it,' Showqi said. 'As far as I

72

know, he has ignored it completely.'

'He doesn't believe it?' Godwin asked.

'He probably believes it to be no more than propaganda put out by the National Front, and as such it is beneath his contempt. It isn't even worth the trouble and expense of an investigation.'

'No man could be that stupid,' Stallard observed.

'He isn't stupid. He is blinded by dreams of glory that can never come true. He knows his dreams can never come true, he knows what is on that tape is not mere propaganda, but his dreams mean so much to him that he will not admit it.'

'Then why did he chuck us off the yacht?' Godwin asked.

The boy shrugged. 'Probably you will find for no more than the reasons he gave Mr Stallard on the phone. Because Stallard upset Andreas, and because the rest of us were uninvited anyway.'

'Or because he, like Hasseler, is making a bloody fortune out of the causeway swindle and he wants Davies to get us before we cruel the deal for him,' Stallard said.

Sigrid Hasseler said, with conviction, 'No. You don't know Jamil Bazarki. That causeway is his entire life. He has lived, always, with no other end in view. It is his god, his heaven. The eighth wonder of the modern world, he calls it. His name is on each end of it, on a brass plaque. Jamil Bazarki. It is his monument.'

They drove on in silence for a time, the road climbing into the south-east through a great rain-forest.

At length, Showqi said, 'Maybe you're right. Maybe my father and Hasseler, for all their noble words, are merely swindlers. But that doesn't bother me. It pleases me. It pleases the National Front. It means a permanent rupture in relations between Jarma and Persia. That makes us happy. But we are not happy about the Bee Sting Deal, and we are not happy about that because we don't know what it is.'

'And if Colonel Davies has his way,' Stallard said, 'you never will.'

73

The end of the road ahead was the horizon, a patch of blue sky blotched by the thick foliage of the high trees. There was not much traffic on the road, a few trucks, one or two natives leading cows, angular, graceful women with bundles on their heads. All the time the car was climbing, and inside it they could feel the effects of altitude on the membranes of their ear-drums.

'Can you tell us in which general direction we're travelling?' Sigrid Hasseler asked Stallard. 'Like, I mean, Cape Town or Cairo?'

Stallard said, 'Cape Town's the nearer. I was thinking of going down there or to Jo'burg. Or across to Rhodesia.'

'No,' Godwin said. 'Not South Africa. Or Rhodesia.'

'Why not?' Stallard asked.

She looked around at Showqi.

'Because of me, Mr Stallard,' the boy said, bitterly. 'In South Africa I have to walk on a different side of the street to you. I am coloured.'

'Oh yes,' Stallard said softly. 'I'd forgotten that.'

'Oh shuttup, Showqi, and stop sulking!' the girl said.

Godwin looked out the window and grinned. She lit a cigarette and then said to Stallard, 'What do you intend to do then? I mean, apart from motoring on *ad infinitum ad nauseam*, do you have any object in view?'

'We've got a bit of a start on them,' Stallard said. 'But it should be easy enough for them to pick up our trail and follow it. If they haven't caught up with us within a day or two, we might be able to stop long enough to get a plane somewhere.'

'Sounds all very nebulous to me,' Godwin said.

'Do you have a better idea?' Stallard asked her.

'No,' she said.

'Well, until you do,' he said, 'don't knock the Establishment.'

'And what if they have caught up with us within a couple of days?'

'Then,' he said quietly, 'we are going to have to defend ourselves.'

74

'The thing is,' Godwin said, 'if Showqi's right and his father is not involved with Hasseler and the Bee Sting Deal, what makes you think that Colonel Davies is here, anyway?'

'What makes you think he's not?' Stallard countered.

'I don't think he's not,' Godwin said, a little stupidly. 'I mean—I'm just not sure.'

'Do you want to go back to Luanda and find out for certain?' Stallard asked her.

She said nothing.

'Because if you do,' he said, 'you can walk. I'm sure as hell not going back.'

'Sorry I spoke,' Godwin said, deflated.

In the middle of the afternoon, they reached the top of the long climb and were driving across the broad Bié Plateau, a sun-baked, fertile plain with a hut or a farm-house here and there upon it, and scrappy patches of shade cast by flat-topped, skeletal acacia trees, or baobab, or patches of low scrub or thorn. It reached away to a misty range of blue hills in the east.

They drove into a place called Malindi consisting chiefly in earth-floored shacks clustered around a long, straggling, slab-sided general store, and a decaying ruin of a rest-house. Ragged hens fluttered about the one street, and a lean-looking dog or two crouched in the shade of some trucks beside the store. On the verandah of the store a couple of degenerate-looking Europeans squatted, seemingly doing nothing other than use up time. Stallard stopped the Caddy behind a dust-caked Land Rover parked by a petrol bowser in front of the store. He turned to the others in the car and said, 'I'm going to get some gear here. I advise the rest of you to do likewise.'

'What sort of gear?' Godwin asked.

'Boots. A hat. You girls should get some long trousers and cover up your legs.' He slid out of the car and slammed the door.

Godwin looked around at the girl in the back seat. 'Now you can see why old Andreas hated his guts.'

'What's bugging him?' Sigrid Hasseler asked.

'Us,' Godwin said. 'He's worried. If Davies kills any of us, it's going to be Stallard's fault. That's how Stallard sees it. You wait for it—as soon as he knows Davies is after us he's going to suggest that we split up, he takes on Davies solo while we get the hell out of it.'

Inside the store, Stallard was making his purchases. He bought provisions for about four days, and six half-gallon water-canteens, as well as a small kerosene stove and four gallons of fuel for it. When the other three entered, he was trying on a hat, a genuine safari-style chapeau with a leopard-skin band.

Godwin laughed and said, 'Get Alan Quartermain.'

Sigrid Hasseler said, 'He looks just like Stewart Granger.'

Stallard muttered an obscenity.

Up a couple of board steps and through an opening hung with plastic strips, was a bar. It was squalid, but offered respectably frozen beer, and while the others were kitting themselves out, Stallard leaned on this bar with a can or two. Apart from the native barman, who was naked down to where his voluminous khaki drill shorts sat upon his hips, there was only one other occupant of the room, and he was a white man. He was sitting at one of the tables, drinking beer, and Stallard scanned him briefly and would have dismissed him but for the object which lay on the table in front of him. It was about two feet long and resembled a tapering snake. There were several stiff, tinily barbed spines projecting from the thin end, the longest of them some three inches. Stallard knew what that was. He had seen Arab boys in the Persian Gulf deftly gaff a ray out of a fish trap, sever the thing's tail at the base, and consign the flapping pancake body back to the sea. Dried and treated with some kind of preservative, the ray-tail is one of the most sadistic and vicious instruments of torture man has ever devised. In Bahrain, where Stallard lived, they were illegal. What sort of man, he wondered, would carry one around with him, openly?

The man's skin was burned the colour of old leather by

76

sun and wind, and he had a flame-red shock of hair and ginger stubble about his jaws. He smoked a home-made, yellow cigarette, and wore a bandolier of 30.30 shells over his right shoulder. His bush jacket and shorts were stained by sweat and dust and he just sat there with his beer, gazing through the open door at the sun-blasted street outside, brushing at flies. He could have been a poacher, a diamond-runner, or even a slaver. But whatever he was, Stallard concluded, he was nothing if not a mean bastard.

Then Sigrid Hasseler came in. She was still wearing the clothes she had left the yacht in, the short, tight shorts and that tight, black tee-shirt without a bra, and the creased-up, lashless eyes of the man at the table took in every inch of every soft, full curve of her. Stallard bought her a beer and then Godwin and Showqi Bazarki joined them. In a corner of the room stood a juke-box. The girl went over to it and began reading the names of the records it played. Then she called back to the bar, 'Has anybody got a coin for this thing?'

The man at the table got to his feet. He said, 'I gotta coin for it,' revealing himself with a thick, tight-lipped accent, to be an Afrikaner. He stood beside Sigrid Hasseler at the juke-box. 'What you want to hear?' he asked.

She shrugged. 'Anything. They all look the same to me.'

Stallard had an uncomfortable feeling about this Afrikaner. He said to his party in general, 'Drink up, we're going.'

'You with him?' the Afrikaner asked the girl. 'Or are you with the kaffir?'

Oh hell, Stallard thought. He did not want trouble here. He did not want a disturbance anywhere along the line which would be remembered.

The girl looked back into the dark, tough face of the Afrikaner. 'I'm with the kaffir.' She smiled at him.

The man grinned at her. 'I like you,' he said softly. 'Which way are you heading?'

'The opposite way to you,' she said, still smiling at him.

'Why don't you come on with me down to Luanda?'

he said. 'We can have some fun down there.'

'Thanks,' Sigrid Hasseler said. 'Next time I want to have some fun with a pig, I'll let you know.'

The fellow laughed and turned from her and went back to his beer at the table. While he drank he was looking straight at Stallard. He put his glass down on the table and, still looking at Stallard, said to the girl, 'Go with your stinking kaffir then.'

Stallard started shepherding his people towards the door. Showqi Bazarki's face was pale, his hands trembling. As they passed by him, the Afrikaner said, 'A goddam bunch of white kaffirs and a real genuine black one. What a combination.'

Outside in the blazing white light, a boy was just screwing the cap back on to the tank of the Cadillac, having filled it from the bowser. The girl said to Stallard, 'I'm sorry about that.'

'Just get in the car!' he snapped at her.

He slid in behind the wheel of the Cadillac. Godwin lit a cigarette and passed it to him as he started the engine and moved off. For a time, both he and his passengers were silent. Godwin looked at him, and at length, Stallard said, 'Did they put all that gear in the car?'

Godwin said, 'Yes. It's in the boot.'

After that, he drove in silence.

At dusk the road on which they were travelling was walled in by great trees. In the high branches, monkeys leapt and swung and birds on broad wings sailed lethargically. The trees rang to the cries of birds and the chattering of monkeys and the lowering sun sent shafts of glowing light down, slantwise, through gaps in the high leaves that were like holes in the roof of a cathedral. On the floor of this vast, still, living theatre of the primeval, the Cadillac moved like an ant. Now it was cool, after the heat of the day, and Stallard dispensed with the car's a.c. unit, and opened the windows.

He said, 'There's a town about twenty miles ahead. We'll need gas there.'

'Are we going to stay there the night?' Godwin asked.

'No. We're going to keep moving.'

'Then let me drive, and you get some sleep.'

'Later,' he said. Soon after refuelling, he turned left, off the main highway onto a dirt road, going north. It was dark now, and in the blaze of the headlights, occasionally, eyes glowed, points of fire in the night ahead. Now they were heading for the Congo border, and a vague plan was forming in Stallard's mind. If they could get into the Congo, and make it to Brazzaville, or Leo, they could fly out from there. That would be the day after tomorrow, if Colonel Davies had not caught up with them by then. If, indeed, Colonel Davies was chasing them. He was beginning to have doubts himself, now.

About midnight he pulled off the road. He was stiff in the joints and cruelly tired. Godwin started up the kerosene stove and cooked some beef and beans and made coffee.

The sounds of chattering and stirring from the high trees were incessant, beyond the buzz and rustle of insects in the darkness, and the inevitable song of mosquitoes. Now and again the chorale was dramatically interrupted by the cough of a leopard.

Stallard took the rifle from its case and cocked and fired the action a couple of times. He loaded five rounds into the magazine and one into the breach, then closed the chamber and applied the safety catch.

Sigrid Hasseler asked him, 'Going hunting?'

'I wish I was,' Stallard said, then looked up at Godwin. 'Are we ready to roll?'

'What *now*?' the girl asked.

'We've got a start on our friends,' Stallard said, 'and I want to keep it that way.'

'What about gasoline?' Showqi Bazarki asked.

'We don't need gas for a hundred miles,' Stallard said. 'Now finish up and get in.'

Godwin said, 'All right, Vic, but I'm driving.'

He did not like surrendering the wheel, but he had to

get some sleep. Half stupid with exhaustion he would be useless to everybody, so he agreed to let Godwin drive. He slapped at a mosquito on his forearm and took up the rifle off the lid of the boot of the car, where he had put it down.

'You know,' the boy said to him, 'I've never fired a gun in anger.'

'Never do,' Stallard answered. 'In anger, you tend to do things you don't mean. And when you fire a gun at a human being, you must mean it.'

7

The heat and the glare of the sun woke him, and he sat up, blinking, and reached for his sun-glasses. He was sore and cramped from sleeping on the seat of the car folded up in the angle of the back-rest and the door-pillar, and there was a taste of dry wool in his mouth. The car was stopped, just off the road. He looked at his watch—11.25. Automatically, he reached for the rifle on the seat beside him, opened the door, and staggered out onto the dusty road. The forest of the night before had given way here to low scrub and stunted, dust-grey thorn, through which the road was cut, die-straight, to the horizon.

Godwin called from away on his right, 'Hi. Feeling better?'

She was there in the shade of an acacia, brewing coffee on the kerosene stove. Showqi was lying on the ground under the tree and there were three tin plates stacked there, off which breakfast had obviously been eaten. They had set up their camp on a patch of smooth sand which, apart from the road, seemed to be the only bit of clear, level ground available. It was in fact the bed of a dry creek, and from the road the ground sloped gently down to it, but on the far side the bank was steep and from its top the terrain continued rising, an easy incline at first, and then an abrupt, rocky, scrub-covered flank going up to a ridge about a hundred feet high. Stallard came down onto the sandy bed and looked about him. 'Where are we?'

Godwin showed him the map. There was a village called Gabriella de Moroto. 'That was the last village,' she said. 'We passed through there about three hours ago.'

'How long have we been stopped?' he asked.

She looked at him belligerently, expecting a reproof. 'About two hours,' she said.

'Christ,' he whispered. 'Why didn't you wake me?'

'If you hadn't needed to sleep, you'd have woken yourself.' She was at work on a can of beans. 'And we're not moving yet, either. You're going to have some breakfast, and some coffee. We're perfectly safe here. You can see anybody coming for miles down that road.'

'I don't want them to get close enough to be able to see them,' he said.

The pan on the cooker sizzled as she tipped the beans and a can of sausages into it. Stallard had to admit that it smelled good and would probably prove worth waiting for.

Then Showqi Bazarki said to Godwin, 'Do you think you should tell him about the plane?'

'What plane?' Stallard demanded.

'A little Cessna,' Godwin said. 'It came down pretty low, had a look at us. Then went back south.'

Hell, Stallard thought, as she handed him a mug of coffee. Still, it would take them a lot longer to catch up by car than it would by plane. Having established the Cadillac's position and heading from the air, they would then, presumably, and hopefully, have to go back and pick up their surface transport. Even so, it would be wise not to linger here, and it would be wise also to change course.

'You think it was them?' Showqi asked.

'Of course it was them,' Stallard said. 'Where's Sigrid?'

'It's her turn at the water-hole,' Godwin said. 'Over there, behind the rocks.'

Stallard scowled in the direction indicated. This was what happened when he relaxed his hold for a couple of hours; the whole goddam organisation disintegrated. 'What's she doing?' he asked.

'Cleaning herself up,' Godwin said. 'You could do with a bit of it too.'

Rubbing his jaw, his hand made a rasping sound in the stubble. But he said, 'As soon as she's finished, we're out of here.'

'Yes,' Godwin said. 'I had an idea we might be.'

The water came down to the pool from a spring higher up on the ridge, and it lay at this spot in a natural bowl of rock. Not long ago, elephant had been here; their droppings lay round about and in places the bush was crushed and their great footprints cratered the mud. But on this hot, golden morning, Miss Hasseler had it all to herself. She stripped and waded in, wallowing in the bite of the cold water. She soaped her body and her hair and washed away the dirt and sweat of the previous night and day. It left her feeling miraculously invigorated.

She came out of the pool and her bare feet wet the hot, dry rock. She was bending to her clothes when there was a sound behind her, a movement of a bush, a soft scrape on the rock. She turned and the sudden, rushing sound of a whip cut the air and a billion blazing needles exploded in her back; the flesh melted and contracted under the murderous bite of the ray-tail, a tightening stripe across her naked back so that her body arched and she felt that her innards must burst out of her with the great quantity of pain that stiffened and bulged in her. Through sudden tears she looked up across her shoulder.

He stood there with his great, dusty boots upon the rock, the red-haired Afrikaner from the bar of the general store at Malindi. In his hand he held the ray-tail whip one swipe of which had cut her open and it hung by his leg, blooded. Down on the mud below a native stood, in ragged shorts, with a rifle slung on his right shoulder, and then she saw the red-haired man look up, and she followed the line of his gaze.

High above, near the top of the ridge, was a man with a rifle. He lay on his front, peering over the spine of the rock, down on the other side of the ridge, where the Cadillac was parked and Godwin and Showqi were sitting on the bed of the dry creek.

It occurred to Sigrid Hasseler to wonder at how silently these men had come.

The Afrikaner wore dark glasses. He looked back from the top of the ridge at the girl on the rock at his feet. She lay whimpering in terror. The Afrikaner's mouth opened a fraction, in a smile, and he raised the ray-tail whip back, over his right shoulder.

The girl drew herself up into a foetal shape, and screamed, and screamed.

Showqi Bazarki flung aside his coffee and was on his feet and running before the girl's screams had really registered with Stallard. When they did, his immediate reaction was to fear that she had been frightened, maybe attacked, by a snake, or a leopard, and he put down his breakfast plate and reached for the F.N., shouting at the boy, 'Wait!'

But the boy was scrambling up the bank of the dry creek. He got a grip on a low thorn bush and pulled himself up and over the top and started running. He had taken two running steps, and Stallard was halfway up the bank after him, when the slug hit him. From the top of the ridge, against the blue sky, came the long, whiplash crack of a rifle shot, echoing for a second, ringing in the still, hot air, and a great, invisible boot kicked Showqi Bazarki in the left side of the chest, lifted him off his feet, and dropped him with a thud in the dust. His body slid down the incline, to the edge of the creek bank, and rolled over, arms and legs flailing like empty stockings in the wind. Godwin screamed and leapt aside to avoid the hurtling body, which dumped and lay still in the sand near where she had been sitting. In the instant in which the sound of the shot reached him, Stallard was in below the level of the creek bank, pressed against the dry gravel wall. He was yelling at Godwin: '*Get down!*'

She came up against the bank beside him, her eyes bulging with horror, staring at the boy's body.

On the kerosene stove, the coffee pot blew billows of steam into the sunlight.

'It's my fault,' Godwin gasped, stupidly, 'it's my fault they caught us . . .'

'Shuttup!' Stallard ordered her, roughly. And then he added, his teeth grit, 'They haven't caught us yet.'

Across the scrub and the rocks they heard the girl screaming again, a wild, hysterical, sobbing scream of pure agony.

Godwin, too, was sobbing now.

Stallard eased his head back from the bank to look up at the top of the ridge, from where the shot had come. He caught a movement up there and fell back below the bank as, again, there came that long, ringing crash of the rifle, and the slug kicked a spout of sand out of the creek bed behind him. The marksman was an expert.

Further along, the creek bed petered out, but there was plenty of cover in the way of scrub and rock. 'Keep your head down and keep behind me,' he told the woman, and then ran, crouched, against the bank, the rifle trailed in his left hand. He stopped, sitting in the sand with his back against a rock, peering around another rock and through some thorn scrub, at the top of the ridge. The range, he estimated, was about a quarter of a mile.

Why was this fellow sitting up there pinning him down? Stallard wondered. There were obviously more than one of them—the one doing the shooting, and the one who was doing something else to Sigrid Hasseler, so at least two. Maybe they were making the girl scream in an attempt to force Stallard into doing something rash, like break cover. So maybe, he thought, he ought to try to force them to do something rash.

The car was thirty feet away, for about ten of which there was no cover.

He said to Godwin, 'Do you think you can get into the car?'

She looked at it. 'Yes,' she said.

It meant she would have to show, for maybe ten seconds, but Stallard had to back his own reflexes against those of the shooter on the ridge. He cranked the back-sight of the F.N. up to five hundred metres, eased off the safety, and drew back on the action until it clicked and held and the gun was cocked.

Sigrid Hasseler's screaming from the water-hole had stopped, which seemed somehow, ominous, and the tension was increased now by another noise, a distant, droning hum, coming closer, increasing in volume. An aircraft engine.

The Cessna came up from the south, and in low along the line of the road to the left of Stallard. It went past forty yards away and with no more than fifty feet of altitude, a great roar and a white blaze of silver in the sun, raising a hurricane of red dust in its slipstream. It was a moment before Stallard understood what was happening—the pilot was inspecting the road preparatory to landing.

He looked at Godwin. 'Colonel Davies has arrived,' he said, and then looked up at the top of the ridge. 'That's what they've been waiting for.'

'So we're surrounded,' she said.

'Honey,' he said, lighting a cigarette, 'you're going to have to get to the car.'

'Yes,' she said. 'Just tell me what to do.'

'They can't afford to let any one of us escape from here. If you get in the car and take off, it might draw them out and give me a shot at them. Before the bastards from the plane get here.'

Her eyes, deep green, wide open, stared at his. She took a quick, nervous pull on her cigarette and wiped her mouth, unnecessarily, on the back of her hand. Then she dropped the cigarette and crushed it with the sole of her shoe. 'All right,' she said.

He said, 'Get down on your belly and crawl around under the scrub there. You'll have to jump for it the last ten or fifteen feet, but I'll be covering you. In the car, keep your head *down*, switch her on and go like hell, back the way we've come. He'll probably get a couple of shots at you, but it would have to be a lucky one to stop you, and while he's trying to hit you. I'll be trying to hit him. Good luck.'

She went, and for a moment he watched her crawling through the bush. Then he moved, upwards, dodging among rocks, keeping low in the scrub and long razor grass. When he saw that she was almost to the end of her cover, he stopped and settled again behind a rock, watching the top of the ridge. He knelt on one knee and took aim. Sweat rivered out of him. He heard Godwin gasp, like a sob, and her feet scrabbling and rushing in the gravel and dry weed and leaves. And then he saw the killer on the ridge, just his head, a small, black mole on the hump of the dinosaur-back high up against the sky, and a sudden white flash which was the sun on the lens of a scope sight.

Stallard's face sweated against the sleek French walnut of the F.N.'s stock, and he drew a breath, exhaled half of it, then held it, slowly squeezing the trigger, while the sweat ran and the heat of the day blazed whitely; there was just the black U of the back-sight and the tiny, standing post of the foresight, centred on that black mole way up there against the blue void of the sky. The F.N. kicked, its blast lashing through the scrub, and almost simultaneously the man on the ridge fired too. But Godwin was in the car. He heard the starter whir, then the engine come alive and rumble softly through its corroded exhaust pipes. He did not look around, but kept the rifle aimed on the ridge.

Then the car took off, the back wheels spinning out sudden geysers of dust and then gripping in the soft gravel and jerking the Caddy forward. She whipped the wheel over, fanning the back end through the dust, swerving, shuddering, to level out on the road and set out south with a slowly crescendoing roar.

Stallard moved again, working uphill through the rocks

and thorn. He had no illusions about where his shot had gone; it had gone close, but it had missed. It had, however, caused the marksman on the ridge also to miss, and that was all he could have asked of it.

He could see the plane now, about a mile up the road; it had landed and been turned around and was taxi-ing back. He looked back at the Cadillac, which was still heading south on the far side of a screen of dust. And then, from quite close to him, on the other side of some rocks, he heard the scratching of heavy boots as a man climbed rapidly around the toe of the ridge, just out of sight. Stallard froze. There were two of them—the shooter on the ridge, and the one who had been doing something to Sigrid Hasseler. He'd heard the car. He was running up from where the pool lay, just the other side of the rocks from Stallard, to see what was going on.

The crunching of the boots on the rock came louder. Stallard crouched among some thorn bushes, gripping the rifle like a pistol in his right hand, watching the top of the rocks twenty feet ahead and above him.

He saw the hat first, the battered, sweat and grease-stained slouch hat with a pale patch on the front where the military insignia had been. And then the fellow was standing there, below the level of the rocks, so that Stallard could see him from the waist up quite plainly. The red-haired Afrikaner from Malindi.

Stallard brought the rifle to his shoulder. The Afrikaner noticed the movement and looked around, and Stallard fired. The slouch hat flew into the air and the man fell back without a sound, half of his head blown off.

The plane had stopped taxi-ing and sat on the road about a hundred yards away and below Stallard's position. He was not so concerned about the plane, however, as he was about the man still above him, on the ridge. From up there, again came the sound of rifle fire. The marksman was still trying to stop the Cadillac, but from the top of the ridge the car, speeding away beyond a wall of dust, was a long shot from an awkward angle. Also, the Caddy carried a lot of superfluous body panelling that made its vulnerable parts none too accessible as targets, and the shooter's only real chance of stopping it was to hit the driver. That too would have been an exceedingly lucky shot, even for a marksman, and the fact that the big car continued on an even keel until it was out of sight indicated that this marksman was not being lucky.

Stallard, by now, had worked himself around into a position from which he could not get a shot at the man above, anyway. He was down at the toe of the ridge, his enemy was among the rocks on its spine, higher up. Here he could hear the trickle of running water, and he knew he was just on the other side of some low rocks from the pool where Sigrid Hasseler had come to bathe. He took another quick look back at the plane.

Three men had descended from it onto the roadway. One, shorter and stouter than the others, looked like Godwin's description of Colonel Davies, and from where Stallard was sitting now he could have killed the Colonel quite easily. It was obvious that these three men were not aware of the situation. They must have seen the Caddy go, and believed that now there was no resistance left here. If so, Stallard thought, good.

Gingerly he raised his head above the level of the rock barrier between him and the pool. Just below him lay the body of the Afrikaner, grotesquely twisted among the rocks, the head a mess of red pulp. Below and beyond this gruesome sight he saw the pool with Sigrid Hasseler's body beside it. She lay on her back with her legs pulled apart and her ankles tied with rough hemp to a couple of scrub roots. Her arms were behind her head so that her head rested on her wrists, which were bound together, also with rough hemp. Maybe she was alive, he could not tell, but the condition of her body suggested what he had imagined had happened to her when he first heard her screaming— she looked as if she had been mauled by a leopard.

She seemed to be alone there, but then he noticed, lower down, cowering at the base of the rock in the mud by the edge of the pool, a native. The man was terrified; but he was unarmed, so Stallard ignored him.

He looked back at the three men who had come out of the plane. They were coming down towards the camp-site at which Stallard's breakfast had been so rudely interrupted. They could wait; he had to get the killer first, the man on the ridge above him.

The rifle reloaded, he started climbing, keeping low, never taking his eyes off the skyline above him.

He was halfway up the humped back of the ridge when, from high among the rocks ahead of him, he heard a distant, ringing shout:

'Get back...'

It was the rifleman up there yelling to the three down below.

Peering between the rocks, Stallard looked down. They were there on the sandy creek bed, under the spread of the acacia tree, grouped around Showqi Bazarki's body. The short, stout man was kneeling, examining the cadaver. At the shout, they looked up; they could hear it, but not well enough to interpret it.

Keep shouting, Stallard silently urged his prey, keep yelling, just once more is all I need...

He wished he had a sling on the rifle, it made climbing damned awkward; but slowly and silently he was making height, a burning ache in the back of his neck from the continual looking up.

The marksman was too wise to shout again. Even so, from the first and only shout, Stallard had placed him well enough. He knew that he was ahead of him; the other man had no idea where his antagonist was.

And then, for a second, Stallard saw the man moving lithely between two rocks.

He got to his feet, and the men in the creek bed below saw him standing against the skyline. They had no idea, of course, that he was not their own man. They saw him move quickly across the tops of the rocks and stop, and a second later they heard the long-echoing blast of a rifle-shot, and the man up there on the rocks dropped down and was hidden from their view.

Showqi Bazarki's killer lay dead at Stallard's feet, an unpleasant sight, his back blown open at very close range by the heavy calibre slug of the F.N. He had been a fairly young man, and his rifle, a .358 magnum Husqvarna with a scope sight, lay beside him. Stallard felt vaguely sick. He sat down against a nearby rock and lit a cigarette and found that his hands were trembling so violently that the simple act became quite a feat in the accomplishing.

From the heights, he gazed down between the boulders at the three men on the sand in the creek bed around his erstwhile breakfasting place. There were now those three swine to be accommodated before he turned his attention to Sigrid Hasseler's plight down by the pool. He could drop one of them from here, but the other two would get in against the bank—and then the stalking and crawling through the scrub would begin again. Stallard now was in no mood for any more of that. He had a feeling that if he had to rejoin battle now, he would lose. In coming this far, he had extended himself to the limit, and he was exhausted. His nerves were playing up, and he felt mentally and physically incapable of carrying on with it.

There was, of course, the temptation to shoot Colonel Davies now. But the idea did not appeal; before Davies died, Stallard wanted to hear him talk—about the Bee Sting Deal. There was one thing he could do from here, on top of the ridge, however, which might at least get the Colonel off his back for the time being.

They were standing down there around Showqi Bazarki's body and one of them was shouting something up at the ridge which Stallard could not interpret. It did not matter, anyway. Between the Colonel and one of his men, a little way in rear of them, stood the kerosene stove on which Godwin's coffee pot was still steaming. Stallard stubbed out his cigarette and reached for the Husqvarna magnum with the scope sight. Sitting comfortably, with his knees up in front of him, his back against a rock, he aimed downwards, focussing the sight firstly on the face of the man he took to be Colonel Davies. The face was in profile, very red and shining with sweat, speaking authoritatively, but in an agitated manner, to the man on his right. Stallard lowered the rifle away from Davies, and the tapered cross-hairs of the sight came upon the little, three-legged stove just behind him. Up a touch, and the rifle was aimed at the stove's copper fuel reservoir. He squeezed the trigger.

The stove exploded with surprising violence, making a flat, dull bang, like a rock being struck with a hammer. The three men fell outwards from the blast, flattening themselves on the sand, and the shirt of one of them was ablaze. The man rolled and thrashed frantically in the sand, but Davies, with astounding agility for his years and build, was up almost as quickly as he had gone down, and running, doubled, back up the far bank of the creek, towards the road. The shirt had been shredded on his back, and was blackened with a show of red through the rents in it. The third man lay as he had dropped, seemingly stunned, but the man who had been on fire was on his feet now. The flames had been extinguished, but he must have been seriously burned and was obviously in great pain. He flung himself about, staggering drunkenly, then fell forward onto the sand and began writhing, trying to crawl away like a snake with a broken back, trying to get to the road; but Stallard doubted that he would make it.

Davies made it, though he too must have been in agony, his back skinned raw by burning kerosene; but shock or sheer guts, or possibly a combination of both, kept him going. Shortly thereafter Stallard heard the Cessna's engine start up, and he was making his way down from the ridge towards the pool when he saw the plane take off, heading south.

Down at the pool, the native who had been crouching by the rock there had now disappeared. But the girl still lay naked, tied, and bleeding. Beside her on the rock lay the bloodied ray-tail whip. Flies crawled in the open cuts on her body. She was not quite unconscious, and moaned, a gargling, rasping sound in her throat, as he began untying her.

About half an hour later, he saw the Cadillac coming back, low down on its back offside where the wheel was running on its rim, the shredded tyre flapping free as it rotated. That boy on the ridge had been a crack-shot.

Stallard looked up, into the high blue dome of the sky, and way up there, in sinister solitude, a small black speck described languid figures of eight.

It was the first of the vultures.

8

The monstrous birds were swinging in to land on the road to the south and a couple had advanced and alighted in the branches of the acacia.

Leaning on the roof of the Cadillac, Stallard looked down into the rear seat where Godwin was trying to dress the cuts and weals on the girl's body. She would live, but she was going to be marked.

Stallard pondered the significance of the Afrikaner's presence here this morning. It must have happened, he surmised, thus: At some time yesterday, Colonel Davies had discovered his quarry had flown Luanda; he had reasoned that they could only have gone by road, so he had sent some scouts to find which road; in due course, one of the scouts had come to Malindi and met the Afrikaner; he had phoned back to Davies in Luanda; Davies had come out in the plane at first light—it was no problem at all to search a couple of hundred miles of open road from the air, now that the Colonel knew what he was looking for, a twelve-year-old, black Cadillac Fleetwood sedan; there weren't too many of those around on these up-country tracks.

Meanwhile, the scout at Malindi and the Afrikaner had discovered a mutual interest in the Cadillac, and so they must have set out together in pursuit. Having spotted the car from the air, Davies had gone back and found these two and put them onto the right road, then taken off again, presumably to go back to Luanda to refuel, or to pick up his two bully boys who had been scouting other roads. Of these two bully boys, one was half-cooked and the other was lying unconscious down there on the bed of the creek, and the vultures were taking a keen interest in both of them.

The Afrikaner had paid; already the great, black birds were standing up there on the rocks at the toe of the high ridge contemplating his remains. The man who had killed Showqi had also paid. But Stallard had a feeling that, for what they had bought, they had not paid enough. Only Colonel Davies could afford to settle that account in full—he, and whomever he was working for.

Now Stallard was going to have to kill the two men who had been hurt by the stove explosion. It was that, or allow them to be eaten alive by vultures. Taking them along in the Cadillac was out of the question, so a bullet in each of their skulls was the only humane way to deal with the situation. At the thought of this, nausea invaded Stallard.

Godwin was tearing up white cotton undergarments to make bandages for the girl's body. The girl lay on the seat of the car, not quite unconscious, moaning softly, and when she was bandaged Godwin put a loose cotton dress on her to cover her. Then Godwin got out of the car and stood beside Stallard.

'There's a bottle of whisky in my bag, if you think it would do her any good,' Stallard said.

'She's in shock, she can't have spirits,' Godwin said, looking with disgust at the vultures floating down from the sky. 'You'll have to bury those bodies, Vic,' she said.

'How can I?' he asked, with an edge of anger, 'how can I dig graves in this gravel with my bare hands?'

She said nothing.

93

Then Stallard asked her, 'Has she been raped?' meaning the girl.

'I don't know,' Godwin said.

He swallowed, freeing his gullet of a constriction. 'I'll have to change this wheel,' he said.

And he had to do the other thing, down on the creek bed. He would change the wheel first.

There were two bullet-holes in the lid of the Cadillac's boot, and one in the roof. The slug that had gone through the roof had smashed through the bulkhead under the dash, and must have missed Godwin by less than a foot. He opened the boot and took out the spare wheel and the jack.

Then, from the creek bed, came a long, mad scream.

Godwin stared. *'One of them is alive!'* she whispered.

The vultures were down there, on the sand, moving in.

Stallard went to the front seat of the car and picked up the rifle.

'What are you going to do?' she asked him.

He was walking down towards the dry creek.

'Vic!' she screamed at him.

He stopped for a moment, looking back at her, and said, 'I've got to.'

After a moment, she looked away, sick, and then staggered around to the other side of the car. He was about to continue on down to the creek when he looked around, towards the sound of an engine coming from the south. A truck was approaching along the road. Stallard ran back to the car, cocked the rifle and waited behind the open car door.

He said to Godwin, 'Get in and get down on the floor.'

The truck drew up behind the Caddy and stopped among billowing dust. It was a big three-tonner with four-wheel drive and a great, cast-iron bumper on the front for ramming its way through bush. The doors opened, and two men stepped down, one on each side. One was a tall, skinny Negro, the other an enormous European dressed in shorts, boots, a checkered sport shirt, and a sweat-stained safari hat. Both men were unarmed.

94

The white man addressed Stallard in German: '*Guten Morgen, mein Herr.*'

Stallard said, 'Do you speak English, *ou français?*'

'Both. Best, I speak English. What is going on here, may I ask?'

Stallard stayed put behind the open car door, the rifle levelled across the ledge of the open window. 'Who are you?' he asked.

'My name is Voltz. I have a plantation near here.' He nodded towards the ridge and the creek bed, where the vultures were continuing to crowd in. 'This is my land. I do not like to see these putrid birds on my land, so I ask you, what is going on here?'

Lowering the rifle, Stallard stepped out from behind the car door, pushing it gently closed. 'Well,' he said, 'we've had a bit of trouble.'

'That would seem to be the understatement of the era,' the German said. 'Are you American?'

'English. My name is Victor Stallard.' Godwin had emerged and was standing on the road on the far side of the car. 'That is Cynthia Godwin, and the girl in there,' he nodded at the back seat of the car, 'is Sigrid Hasseler. She's hurt. There are two men down there in the waadi, also hurt. I was just going down to—do something about them, when you turned up.'

The man called Voltz was as tall as Stallard and half as heavy again. He had a large, square jaw covered in black stubble, and a wide, black moustache. Silently, he looked back into Stallard's eyes for a moment, and he got the message—he knew what the something was that Stallard had been going to do about the two men in the waadi. But he did not comment. He just said, 'You want some help, my friend?'

'Yes,' Stallard said. 'I do.'

Voltz looked at the half-jacked-up rear end of the car, at the shredded tyre, and at the slug-holes punched in the lid of the boot. 'You are police?' he asked Stallard.

'No.'

'Were they police?' he asked, and jerked his head in the direction of the ridge.

'No,' Stallard said.

A faint, ironic humour came into Voltz's eyes. *'Une guerre privée*, huh?'

'You might call it that,' Stallard said.

Godwin had her passport in her hand. 'Look, Mr Voltz,' she said, 'I'm a journalist, I represent the London *Daily World*. We're not criminals.'

Voltz considered the passport more out of courtesy than curiosity. Then he handed it back to her. 'Come on,' he said to Stallard, 'before those stinking birds get at them.'

They brought the two wounded men up and lay them in the bed of Voltz's truck. Voltz pulled two shovels out of the truck and tossed one to his man. To Stallard he said, 'We will bury the others. You carry on changing your wheel.'

He went off, followed by the African.

In the back of the truck, one of the injured men was moaning. He had hit his head on a rock as he fell and there was a gash in the top of his scalp and the blond hair was matted in a great clot of dry, black blood; but he was still alive. When he regained consciousness, he would have a headache; but he might be a problem, Stallard thought.

As he changed the wheel on the Cadillac, Godwin asked him, 'What do you make of this man Voltz?'

'We'll have to trust him,' Stallard said. 'We don't have much alternative for the moment. I don't fancy tearing off north into the Congo with the girl in the condition she's in. And we might have trouble crossing the frontier.'

'What do you mean?'

'I doubt it, but Davies might have put in the poison for us with the Angolan authorities, just to keep us pinned down here long enough for him to get another crack at us.'

Godwin watched the big German and the African working on a grave for Showqi Bazarki down in the sand of the dry creek bed. She said to Stallard, 'Why didn't you kill Davies when you had the chance, Vic?'

96

He had finished changing the wheel. In the great heat he was soaked with sweat. He reversed the hydraulic valve on the jack and with a soft hiss it lowered the fresh tyre onto the road. Stallard straightened up.

'Maybe I should have,' he whispered. 'Give me a cigarette.'

The Cadillac followed Voltz's truck back down the road. About half a mile south of the ridge, they passed two Land Rovers, parked and almost hidden in a grove of eucalypts, just off the road. One of the vehicles both Stallard and Godwin recognised as having been parked outside the general store at Malindi on the previous afternoon; it had belonged to the red-haired Afrikaner. This is how the Afrikaner and the marksman had come so silently up to the ridge, they had left their vehicles here and stalked north, through the scrub, on foot.

Eventually Voltz turned onto a dusty, rain-rutted, gravel wheel-track, heading almost due west, and Stallard followed him. On either side, cultivated fields of coffee were laid out as far as the jungle to the south and, to the north, a range of low, blue hills. They met a big, dusty Ford pick-up going in the opposite direction, and stopped while Voltz conversed with the driver of the pick-up for a time. Then they proceeded.

Beyond the coffee fields, the scrubby, dusty nature of the land gave way to broad meadows of bright green maize, criss-crossed by irrigation pipes, and tall, shady eucalypts lined the road. On the drive up to the house they passed neat, white-painted out-buildings, a goat-pen, a corral with two horses in it, a barn overhung by a great tree in the shade of which about six big, sleek Saluki dogs lay, panting in the heat.

The homestead was a sprawling bungalow surrounded by lovingly tended flower gardens. As the two vehicles drew up in the yard, a woman emerged from behind the fly-screened front door and stood on the verandah, wiping her hands in her apron, watching the truck, and the car that had followed it in. Voltz descended from the truck and signalled to Stallard to come with him. They went over to the verandah and Voltz said, 'This is Mardi, my wife.'

She was about half the size of the big German, a pleasant little squirrel of a woman, and she smiled at Stallard and held out her right hand. 'My English is not so good as Heini's,' she said, 'but you are welcome.'

Stallard shook her hand and thanked her.

Then Voltz and his wife conversed for a time in German. At the end of it, Mardi Voltz said to Stallard, 'Okay, you bring the girl into the house and take the men to the bunkhouse over there, huh? And I call the doctor.'

'I'm not sure about the doctor,' Stallard said. 'The men were hurt by a kerosene stove exploding—that could have been an accident. But the girl has been whipped and possibly raped. The doctor might feel obliged to inform the police about that, and I do not want the police involved.'

Voltz scowled. 'Whipped, you say?'

The woman looked pained and slightly sick.

Voltz said, 'You have killed the pig that did this, Stallard?'

Stallard said softly, 'Yes. I killed him.'

'And these two.' He indicated the truck in which the two injured men were lying. 'They were with that pig?'

'It's a long story, Mr Voltz,' Stallard said. 'I'll explain it to you later.'

'Yes,' Voltz said. 'That's for sure.' He looked at his wife. 'Forget the doctor,' he said, 'for the time being. We'll see how badly these people are hurt and call the doctor only if it is absolutely necessary. Come, Mr Stallard, we will attend first to the girl.'

Later in the afternoon, fed, bathed, and wearing a change of clothing, Cynthia Godwin stood on the verandah of Voltz's bungalow and looked out across the green fields to the hills in the west. The hills now were deep purple edged with electric gold, and the sky above them a vast wash of scarlet paling to lemon in this African sunset, and it was difficult, in the stillness and peace of her environment now, for Godwin to remember what had happened

98

that morning in the bright heat and the dust and the wild thorn scrub and rocks, just over there on the other side of those hills.

Stallard looked a hell of a lot better for a bath and a shave and a suit of clean clothes. He came onto the verandah, ice cubes tinkling in a tumbler of whisky and soda that he carried, and Voltz followed him, also with a drink. Seeing Godwin there, Voltz stopped in the doorway and asked her, 'Ah, Miss Godwin, will you have a drink?'

'Yes, please, Mr Voltz. Vodka,' she said.

He relayed the order to the house-boy inside. They sat in great wicker chairs around a small wicker table with a plate-glass top, and watched the splendour of the sunset. Then, rending the stillness, the trumpet of a bull elephant echoed across the long, flat fields, and Voltz cursed in German.

Then he said, in English, 'Hear him? There is a herd of the *schweinhunds* up there. I have some men out trying to keep them out of my pineapples, but if they come in I will have to go up there and shoot that bull.'

'This must be a good life you have here, Mr Voltz,' Godwin said.

'Since the war, it has been good here,' Voltz agreed. 'During the war, I was a prisoner, of the goddam English.'

'You don't look that old,' Stallard said, truthfully.

'Thank you, my friend. But I'm fifty-two. Me and my little Mardi, we are grandparents, you know. We have a son, a graduate of Frankfurt, a petroleum engineer, and he is working in Trinidad now. And we have a daughter who is a translator for the Americans at Frankfurt, and who is engaged to marry a goddam Yankee.'

'You don't seem too pleased about that,' Godwin smiled.

'Ah, he is all right, he is just a boy, you know? He came down here and told me all about what I was doing wrong here and how I could fix the place up to make real money and set up an hotel here and bring tourists in and all, you know how these goddam Yankees are. Maybe when I'm dead, I'll give him a chance down here.' Then the German's

99

big, dark face became grave. 'He is impetuous, like the boy you told me about, whom we buried this morning, Mr Stallard.'

Stallard struck a match and applied the flame to a cheroot gripped between his teeth. As he exhaled blue smoke, he looked worried. 'I wish you hadn't got involved in this, Voltz,' he said.

'You think your Colonel Davies is going to try and kill me, now, huh? Well, my friend, Colonel Davies might find this old German is a damn sight tougher than he looks.'

Stallard said, 'Your wife isn't all that tough, though.'

'By God, I'll . . .'

'No,' Stallard said. 'The Colonel is no respecter of the proprieties, friend. He'll get at you any way he damn well can.'

'I'm not scared of Colonel Davies, Stallard,' Voltz said. 'Just leave it at that, huh? I've got a plane here. Tomorrow morning I'll fly you to Brazzaville.'

'If the girl's well enough to travel,' Stallard said. 'I can't leave her here.'

'You think she will not be safe here?'

'I know that if she stays here, nobody will be safe here, and that includes you and your wife.'

Voltz was angry now and with his great, bunched fist he thumped the arm of his chair. 'I can look after my own!' he said.

'No,' Stallard said. 'Not against Davies. What do you do if he burns down your house? Fires your crops? Slaughters your beasts, blows up your trucks—kills your wife and your servants and your men? You've got roots, Heini, he can attack you on so many fronts and he can cripple you without ever touching you physically. Me, he can only attack me as I stand. Please do it my way.'

'And what is your way?' Voltz asked, belligerently.

'The girl will have to come with me when I go.'

'Okay; and what else?'

'Something's got to be done about those two down in the bunk-house.'

'You mean like kill them? In cold blood? Two helpless men?'

'As soon as they're no longer helpless, Heini, they'll bring Davies here, and Davies will have no scruples about killing *you* in cold blood.'

Voltz said, 'Could I try one of your cigarillos?'

'Of course,' Stallard said, and passed one across. He carried them loose in the breast pocket of his shirt.

Lighting the black weed, Voltz looked at the woman. 'What do you think, Miss Godwin?'

She said, 'I have to agree with Vic, Mr Voltz.'

'Kill them?' He raised his bushy black eyebrows at her.

She looked at Stallard. 'Of course, if you'd killed Davies this morning when you had him in your sights, this problem would never have arisen,' she said.

'That, presumably, would have been killing a man in cold blood,' Voltz said, also looking at Stallard. 'And you couldn't do it.' He puffed on Stallard's cheroot, looked at it and grimaced, and picked a scrap of weed off the tip of his tongue. 'It takes a kind of reptilian insensitivity to kill a man in cold blood, Victor. You don't have it, I don't have it, so what do we do? Do I order one of my boys to kill them with an assegai?'

'I'm going to have to force myself, Heini.'

'Look, Vic.' Volt leaned forward. 'I agree you should take the girl with you when you go; but neither of those men is going to be able to leave here for at least a week. I have a prison here, a jail, that I put the boys in when they need some cooling off. It is a concrete box with walls two feet thick and a steel door. I can put them in that if they begin to look dangerous within a week, and from what you've told me of your friend Davies, he is not the sort of man who will hang around in a place like Luanda for a week on the off-chance of picking up a lead as to where you've gone. Now is he?'

Stallard left his chair and stood on the edge of the verandah, looking out across the darkening fields at the sunset's fading glow. This German, he realised, was a brave and

101

humane man; there should be no more talk of killing.

At length, Stallard said, 'All right, Heini. You win.'

'You leave them here?'

Stallard nodded.

'Good. And do not worry, Victor,' Voltz said. 'I am not a fool.'

The fly-screen door opened and Mardi Voltz joined them on the verandah. Her husband, chivalrously, got to his feet while she was seating herself.

Stallard sat down again at the table and said to Mardi Voltz, 'How's the girl?'

'She's unhappy,' the woman said, 'but physically, not too bad.'

'Will she be fit to travel in the morning?' Voltz asked.

'I suggest you ask her that,' his wife said.

The dinner gong sounded warmly in the twilight.

'Ah!' Voltz said, and grinned at his wife, 'and what have you cooked us?'

'It just a *bernerplatte*,' she said.

The meal, however, was copious and excellent and accompanied by a fine wine. At the table Voltz abandoned the thunderous Teutonic mantle he had worn during the cocktail hour and turned all light and hearty. 'We should have guests more often, Mardi. We grow like two cabbages out here in the bush alone. We are immersed in Wagner and Strauss, we do not know what is the music in Vienna and in Munchen now . . .' The mention of Munchen set him off. '*Mein Gott,* Stallard, have you ever been to the Hofbrauhaus?'

Stallard nodded. 'Once or twice,' he said.

Voltz started singing *In Munchen*.

His wife protested, 'Heini, you are turning the wine to vinegar.'

The big man laughed and banged the table. 'Look at you, woman,' he said to his wife, 'you don't know what the women in Paris are wearing now, look at Miss Godwin; you would never have thought to buy a dress like that!'

Mardi Voltz said, 'Miss Godwin is a beautiful young

102

woman, Heini, and she is perhaps twenty-five years younger than I am.'

Truthfully, Godwin said, 'You're too kind, Mardi.'

'No,' the woman said. 'When I was twenty-five years younger, I was beautiful too. I was fashionable, I was sexy. He brings me out here into the middle of the jungle and lets me grow old. What does he expect?'

Voltz laughed, pouring the end out of a bottle and signalling the boy to bring more. 'Stallard, I have a good woman here,' he said. 'And so have you. You want to marry her.'

'She won't have me,' Stallard said.

'It would be marrying beneath me,' Godwin said.

Mardi Voltz grinned at her.

'You know, Stallard,' Voltz said, 'for a man who was threatening to blow my guts open this morning, I've come to like you.'

'Threatening to do what?' Mardi asked.

'He was goddam-well going to kill me this morning when I first met him,' Voltz said. 'He had a gun aimed at my belly and I knew that if I put a foot wrong he would blow my goddam guts open.'

'Heini!' his wife admonished him, 'this is no language for the dinner table.'

'It is crude language, but it is true,' Voltz said.

Mardi looked at Stallard. 'Were you going to kill him?' she asked.

Stallard masticated food, slowly, as if it had gone bad in his mouth. He swallowed, then took a sip of wine. 'I thought he might be someone else,' he said, quietly.

'Like the man who whipped the girl?' the woman asked.

'Someone like that,' Stallard said.

'The world is not full of such people, Mr Stallard,' she said, softly.

He looked at her, at her large, soft, brown eyes. 'I know, Mardi,' he said.

'Goddam this wine,' Voltz said. 'After dinner, Stallard, we will have some beer. Dortmunder. It is in cans, I can't get it draught out here, but it is cold and it is beer.'

103

'I'd like to take a look at those two in the bunk-house,' Stallard said, 'just to make sure they're not going to bother us during the night.'

'Sure, we'll have a look at them,' Voltz said.

Mardi Voltz leaned towards Godwin, smiling. 'Do you play canasta?'

'Yes,' Godwin said with sudden enthusiasm, 'and so does Victor.'

'No!' Voltz protested. 'We do not want to play goddam cards!'

'Yes, we do, Heini,' his wife said softly. 'Miss Godwin wants to play, and so do I, and so does Mr Stallard; and after this somewhat—uncivilised day—we are all in need of a civilised pursuit to end it.'

In the morning, after a substantial breakfast, Sigrid Hasseler felt well enough to rise from her bed. Her wounds were painful, but she appeared to have recovered from the shock to which she had succumbed as a result of her experience of the previous day. Her body was covered with prominent, red weals margined with blue-black bruising, and in three or four places where the whip had broken the skin the cuts had been dealt with by Mardi Voltz, with antibiotic ointment, gauze, and neat strips of plaster in a way that would have done credit to a professional healer. Cynthia Godwin and Mardi Voltz helped her dress, but she refused to wear any undergarment. It was understandable in that anything tight on her body would have caused her considerable distress, but Mardi was of the opinion that, for the sake of propriety, a young lady should be prepared to endure a certain amount of agony.

'You English are obscene,' Mrs Voltz pronounced.

'Nobody's going to see anything,' the girl said, 'except perhaps Victor, and he's seen it already.'

'No, he hasn't,' Mardi Voltz said. 'He didn't look. He's a gentleman.'

Godwin laughed. 'I've heard him called some funny things,' she said, 'but never before ...'

'No,' the other woman protested, 'you misjudge him. He is a gentleman.'

With a certain amount of pride, Heinrich Voltz wheeled out his twin-engined Beechcraft Buccaneer, and set about checking her oil, hydraulics, and electrics, while Stallard was loading his and the two women's baggage. Mardi kissed Godwin and the girl, but she shook hands with Stallard and drew him aside. 'When you and Cynthia have your problems solved—about this Colonel Davies—you will come back to us,' she said, 'for a long holiday.'

He smiled and said, 'Thank you, Mardi.'

'You're good for Heini,' she said. 'He likes you.'

Stallard said, 'We'll be back.'

'Hey, Stallard!' Voltz was standing on the wing of his plane. 'What you want me to do with those guns?'

Stallard had left the rifles, the F.N. and the Husqvarna magnum, in the house. As he climbed up into the plane, he said, 'Keep them oiled, Heini.'

A little under three hours later, they landed at Brazzaville in the Congo. Voltz came into the transit lounge for a last drink with them, and while the drinks were coming Stallard found out about onward flights. He came back to the table, sat down, and lit a cigarette. Then he looked at Sigrid Hasseler. 'How are you feeling, honey?' he asked her.

'Fine,' she said, but she was looking pale.

'There's a flight to Cape Town in two hours' time,' he said. 'Feel up to it?'

'Of course I do,' she said.

'Why Cape Town?' Godwin asked.

'Because late today or early tomorrow, the *Shaheen* is going to dock there. They didn't bunker at Luanda, I'm almost certain, so they'll have to stop at Cape Town, for fuel—also, to take on a passenger.' He looked at the girl. 'Virginia Hasseler,' he said. 'I want her to see her daughter.'

'Well, her daughter doesn't want to see Virginia Hasseler,' the girl said, with feeling.

'You don't have to see her,' Stallard said. 'Close your eyes. Two minutes is all it will take. I just want her to see what they did to you.'

The girl looked at Godwin, near to tears, and Godwin gripped her hand. 'You'll be all right,' Godwin said to her.

The girl looked down at the table, and after a moment she looked up at Heinrich Voltz. There were tears coming out of her eyes, running on her sunburned face.

'Go with Stallard,' Voltz said to her. 'Trust him.'

Wiping away her tears, she nodded mutely.

'Okay?' Stallard asked her. 'Cape Town?'

Again, more slowly, she nodded.

9

At about eleven o'clock the following morning, at his hotel in Riebeeck Square, Stallard was informed by the Cape Town port authority that the *Shaheen* had just docked.

He hung up the phone and said to Godwin and Sigrid Hasseler, who were in the room with him, 'They've made it.'

'And without Lord Nelson at the helm,' Godwin said. 'However did they do it?'

'I suppose Andreas is out to prove himself,' Stallard said, and added quite unashamedly, 'or they've had pretty good weather. But if I'd had her, she'd have been cleared out of here twelve hours ago.'

'How Britannia ever got to rule the waves without you, Victor,' Godwin said, 'is nothing short of a bloody miracle.'

He grinned and lifted the phone again. He sent an urgent rush telegram to Mrs Virginia Hasseler aboard the yacht, specifying that the telegram be marked 'personal'; and about two hours later the phone rang again.

Stallard answered it. 'Mrs Hasseler?'

106

'This is Virginia Hasseler. Who is that?'

'Victor Stallard.'

'You sent me a telegram this morning?'

'Yes. I'm in Cape Town and Sigrid is here with me. Here she is.'

He held the receiver up to the girl, and she said, without any enthusiasm whatever, 'Hallo, Mummy.'

There was a babble from the other end of the line. Then the girl said, 'I'm all right, Mummy. Here's Mr Stallard.'

When he put the receiver back to his ear, the woman on the line was saying, urgently, 'Sigrid, wait! Sigrid!'

He said, 'If you want to see her, this is what you do. There's a bar on the Heerengracht, the Tropicana. Go there at seven o'clock this evening and show your passport to the manager, he'll give you a sealed envelope. In it is the address we're at. But you'll have to be alone, Mrs Hasseler, or he won't give you the envelope.'

'But I think Andreas intends to sail this afternoon.'

'Then you'll just have to miss the boat,' he whispered, angered, 'won't you?' and hung up.

Godwin went to the Tropicana bar with the sealed envelope, explained to the manager there what he had to do, and rewarded him financially for his trouble. At dusk, Stallard had a shower, shave, and dressed in a light grey suit, dark blue shirt, and black silk tie.

'Good-bye, ladies,' he said, and kissed them, and Godwin told him to please be careful—Virginia Hasseler had had time to contact Davies since she had spoken with Stallard on the phone. Then he went.

In the soft, cool half-light of the Tropicana, the cocktail hour was just beginning. Ladies and gentlemen lounged about in big, brocaded easy chairs, or stood an inch deep in the pile of the carpet and leaned on the leather-padded bar. They were all immersed in witty conversation, dry martinis, and their own questionable importance. Behind the bar, the wall was plated with large mirror tiles. Stallard occupied a stool in a dark corner, took delivery of a large whisky with ice and soda, lit a cheroot, and waited.

107

She arrived about ten past seven and stopped at the far end of the bar. She spoke to the bartender, who called the manager for her. The manager was a tall, big-boned, though dapper Dutchman, and Stallard watched him examine the woman's passport, and then hand over the envelope to her. Immediately she had the envelope, she left, and Stallard followed her. He watched her cross the pavement and get into a waiting taxi, and while she was opening the envelope to find out where to go, Stallard ascertained that she was alone. Then he crossed the pavement, opened the cab door, and slid into the seat beside her. 'The Pretorius,' he told the driver. The woman had taken a blank sheet of paper from the envelope, and she looked, puzzled, from the paper to Stallard.

'Just a precaution,' he explained. 'I'm Stallard.

'Are we going to see Sigrid now?' she asked him.

'Yes.' He nodded.

In the sitting-room of the suite at the Pretorius, Sigrid Hasseler and her mother stared at each other for a moment before the woman, tears in her eyes, ran to the girl and embraced her. But the girl pushed her away.

'My back hurts,' she said.

'What's wrong with your back?' the woman asked.

Godwin said, 'Come into the bedroom, Mrs Hasseler.'

The women went into the bedroom. Stallard lit a cheroot and poured a large whisky, which he took out onto the balcony. Once, from the bedroom, he heard a muffled shriek, and then Godwin and Virginia Hasseler emerged, the latter holding a handkerchief to her mouth. As if in shock, she sat dumbly on the edge of a chair.

Godwin took her a drink. 'They killed Showqi?' the woman asked.

Stallard nodded. ' "They" being Colonel Davies. Whom I believe you know.'

The woman's expression combined incredulity and pain.

Stallard went on: 'We were set up for it, either by Jamil Bazarki or by your husband. Jamil ordered us ashore at Luanda, and the Colonel was waiting for us. Why, I don't

108

know, but I'd like to, Mrs Hasseler.'

The woman sat hunched, forlorn, staring at Stallard. 'I honestly don't know, Mr Stallard,' she said.

'There was a man in New York,' Stallard said. 'He was murdered too. He made a tape recording, which Showqi played for me and which seemed to go some way towards an explanation. Have you heard this tape?'

'You mean Charles Schreiber?' she asked.

He nodded. 'That's the name.'

Virginia Hasseler looked at Godwin and breathed a great sigh. Then she said, 'That man—Schreiber, I can tell you about him and his tape. He did work on the Jarma Causeway job, as he says, and he did have figures to back up the lies that he told on that tape. I'll tell you why they were lies.' She sipped a drink, then took a gold lighter from her purse and looked around for a cigarette.

Godwin handed her a packet of Kent.

With her cigarette lit, Virginia Hasseler said, 'The Jarma Causeway job was costed at 120 million dollars, and all things being equal that is what it would have cost to build that bridge exactly according to specification. But all things were not equal—in assessing that cost we overlooked the existence of the Jarma National Front, Showqi Bazarki's group. From the beginning, we could not get local labour; the National Front had threatened any Jarmani who worked on the causeway with reprisals, either against his person or his family. So we had to bring Persians across; then the National Front started harassing them as well. All along there were delays, sometimes running into weeks, in one instance into months, and of course costs spiralled. In the end we were faced with three alternatives: abandon the project; multiply the original cost estimate by three and pay up with a smile; or go ahead, on the basis of the original estimate, and get some kind of a bridge, any kind of a bridge, built. The third of these alternatives, was the only viable one and the only one we could choose.'

She ashed her cigarette. Stallard was pouring himself another drink.

109

'I'll have one too,' Godwin said to him. 'Mrs Hasseler?'
'Please,' the woman said.
'Carry on,' Stallard said to her.
'So we had to start cutting costs,' she said. 'As Schreiber points out on the tape, instead of a six-lane highway, we had to make it four lanes; this considerably lessened the weight of the structure, of course, so that pylons could be spaced farther apart. Second-rate materials had to be used, Schreiber again points out—corners had to be cut all along the line, just as Schreiber says. But there were no fortunes made out of it, Mr Stallard. Even with all the cost-pruning, that bridge cost every cent of the 120 million dollars that were budgeted for it, and a little more on top. My husband has had to take legal advice on putting the Jarma Causeway Company into liquidation. The job, if it hadn't been for his other financial interests, would have ruined him.'

'So you've got a causeway that's going to collapse as soon as the first big wind hits it,' Stallard said.

'It's not quite as vulnerable as that,' the woman said. 'It will stand adequately for two or three years, and this is all Jamil Bazarki wanted. He sold his ideas to the Iranian Government, and he sold them to my husband—just get a bridge, of any description, laid down, was his argument, to establish the fact as unassailable that Jarma is now a province of Persia, and he is confident that the benefits which will accrue from the causeway over the next five years will justify its being strengthened and enlarged. Schreiber took all these pieces of paper he has, all his facts and figures, to a New York newspaper, and tried to sell them what he called "an exposé of one of the greatest swindles of all time". The newspaper, naturally, took the matter up with the Iranian Government, and, through my organisation, with Jarma. We invited the paper to send its own team of engineers and writers out to the Gulf to do a story at first hand on the causeway. They came, they got a bit of a story —which was published in the *New York Weekend News*, page seventeen, on April 20th last, and they did not buy Mr Schreiber's exposé.'

110

'Why was Schreiber murdered, then?' Stallard asked.

'Are you suggesting that Davies did that too?' she asked.

Stallard shrugged. 'Schreiber was shot, I understand . . .'

'People are being shot in New York every day of the week, Mr Stallard, how do I know why Schreiber was murdered?'

'Well, a man was murdered in London, Mrs Hasseler. Straight after he'd visited you and your husband and mentioned the Bee Sting Deal. After his speech about the causeway, on the tape, Schreiber appended a little sort of postscript in which he describes how he found out that there was such a thing as the Bee Sting Deal in existence, and propounded a theory as to what it might entail. Two men who have learned of the existence of the Bee Sting Deal and met violent deaths soon afterwards. What does that mean, Mrs Hasseler?'

'I don't know,' she said. 'This postscript on the tape that you describe, it wasn't on the tape that I heard.'

'The tape that you heard had been edited.'

'What was his theory, anyway?'

'It was this,' Stallard said. 'Assuming that your husband had made so much money out of the causeway swindle, when the causeway falls down, as it must do eventually, he's going to have some awkward questions to answer. In anticipation of those questions, he's going to destroy the causeway with explosives at some time in the near future. He's even got a Russian saboteur in Jarma, working out how it can best be done. That was Schreiber's theory of the Bee Sting Deal.'

The woman shook her head. 'It's utter nonsense.'

'Your daughter told me,' Stallard said, 'that somebody from the Russian Embassy had called on your husband in London. Do you deny that?'

The woman said nothing. She sat tight-lipped.

'You don't deny it?' Stallard prompted.

Still, the woman remained silent.

'What I don't understand,' Godwin said, puffing agitatedly on a cigarette, 'is how Tod Spencer came to be murdered so soon after leaving your house in London, Mrs Hasseler. Can you explain that?'

'Davies is a friend of the family,' Stallard said to Godwin. 'Remember?'

'Davies was visiting us that night, yes,' Mrs Hasseler said.

'You're either a liar, Mrs Hasseler,' Godwin said, bitterly, 'or a bloody fool.'

The woman stood up and turned her back on the room. 'Perhaps I'm a bloody fool,' she whispered.

'You must admit,' Stallard tried reasoning with her, 'that the evidence against your husband is pretty damning. There's Schreiber's story. There's the Russian who visited him in London, and the Russian we are told is in Jarma. You admit you know Davies; and there's the murder of Tod Spencer. These phenomena are somehow linked, and either you know how, or you are a fool, Mrs Hasseler. A very big fool. And you're going to stay here until you've explained yourself satisfactorily one way or the other.'

Virginia Hasseler just said, doggedly, 'I know nothing at all about the Bee Sting Deal.'

Godwin lit another cigarette. 'I can make her talk,' she said.

Stallard looked at her.

Godwin stood up. To Virginia Hasseler, she said, 'Do you know who sent Tod Spencer to see you in London?'

'Yes,' the other woman said. 'I know.'

'Who?' Godwin asked.

'Somebody called Mrs Black.'

'That's right. And who is Mrs Black?'

'She's a madam,' Virginia Hasseler said, with distaste.

'Davies told you this?'

Mrs Hasseler nodded.

'What's Mrs Black's interest in you?' Godwin asked. 'Do you know?'

'I have no idea,' the other woman said, 'and so far we've been unable to find out.'

'Shall I tell you?'

112

Virginia Hasseler looked at Godwin, staring into the green eyes, knowing she was about to hear something dreadful, unable to prevent herself from hearing it. 'Yes,' she whispered. 'Tell me.'

'She's Sigrid's mother,' Godwin said.

That took a moment to register with Mrs Hasseler. Then, slowly, her eyes that had been staring at Godwin, lost focus, her mouth hung open, stupidly. 'What did you say?' she whispered.

'I said Mrs Black is Sigrid's mother,' Godwin told her.

Pain, and then anger, came into Virginia Hasseler's eyes, and suddenly she screamed: '*I* am Sigrid's mother!'

'You're not,' Godwin said, cruelly. 'Mrs Black is her natural mother.'

The woman stood speechless, staring in horror and in wonder at Godwin. She swayed as if she were going to faint, and Stallard caught hold of her elbow to steady her.

Mercilessly, quietly, Godwin went on: 'Sigrid, of course, doesn't know. But she's going to. Tonight, unless you start talking and making sense.'

'*No!*' the woman screamed.

The bedroom door opened and Sigrid stood there in her nightie. 'What on earth are you doing to her?' she inquired.

'Darling!' the woman gasped, and tried to go to the girl, but Stallard held her.

'Get back into bed,' he told the girl. 'Shut the door and go to sleep.'

She looked at Virginia Hasseler for a moment, her face blank, then she withdrew into the bedroom, and the door closed.

Godwin said to Mrs Hasseler, 'What was Davies doing at your house the night Tod Spencer came there?'

Stupidly, as though half drugged, the woman said, 'He was looking for Showqi Bazarki.'

Stallard lowered her back into the chair she had been occupying.

'Go on,' Godwin said to her.

'The National Front movement was outlawed in Jarma.

113

As its leader, Showqi was wanted by the police. As the Chief of Police, Davies was looking for him.'

'To shut him up about the Bee Sting Deal,' Stallard said. 'And he accidentally heard Spencer mention it, and Spencer died while Davies was torturing him to make him talk. Now what do *you* know about the Bee Sting Deal, Mrs Hasseler?'

In fear, the woman looked up at him. 'Nothing,' she whispered. 'I swear to you I know nothing.'

'What about this explosive?' he asked her. 'On the tape, Schreiber says that there are two hundred pounds of TNT hermetically sealed into the bases of the pylons on the Jarma Causeway.'

'That's a natural enough precaution, surely,' the woman said. 'Iran is the only buffer that exists between Jarma and the Soviet Union. The causeway, which makes Jarma geographically a part of the Persian mainland, removes the buffer.'

'But surely, if you were cutting costs, such a precaution would be classed as a luxury you could ill afford.'

'The compartments containing the explosive were pre-fabricated in Germany,' the woman explained. 'By the time we found we were having to cut costs, it would have meant an added expense to have excluded them.'

Stallard paced the floor, smoking. Godwin was pouring more drinks. She handed him one and he took it, absently, without thanking her. He was trying to marshal his facts, trying to think of the correct question to put to Virginia Hasseler, because he just was not getting through to this woman, she was not giving him the information he felt she could give him.

He started at the beginning again. 'When Sigrid first disappeared,' he said to Mrs Hasseler, 'in France, on her way back to the Sorbonne, you knew where she was, didn't you?'

The woman sighed. 'We didn't know where she was. We were fairly sure that she was with Showqi, but we didn't know where.'

'Then you got a letter from Showqi.'

'We didn't know it was from Showqi, but we guessed.'

Then Godwin stepped in. 'The letter said: Call off the Bee Sting Deal, or you will never see her again. Right?'

The woman nodded. 'That letter was the first that either my husband or I had heard of the Bee Sting Deal.'

'The information passed to Mrs Black by one of your domestic staff,' Godwin said, 'was that you and your husband were arguing about the letter.'

'We were not arguing about it, we discussed it. The spy in the house probably heard either me or Conrad reading the letter aloud. We couldn't make head or tail of it, but we certainly weren't arguing about it.'

'All right,' Stallard said. 'Now what about the Russians?'

The woman drew on her cigarette. She was red-eyed and her face was still wet from her tears. The cigarette trembled between her fingers. 'Can I have my daughter back?' she whispered.

'When you've answered all the questions!' Stallard snapped at her. 'Now what about the Russians who visited your husband in London.'

Breathing deeply, Virginia Hasseler started to talk again. 'The Jarma Causeway fiasco left Conrad practically bankrupt. Quite out of the blue, a man from the Russian Embassy in London visited him. The Russian knew all about the Jarma Causeway Company's financial problems. He knew exactly how much money Conrad needed to get himself out of trouble, and that is what he offered—if Conrad would agree to leave all the causeway company plant in Jarma for a period of six months after the completion of the causeway construction programme. Nothing else, all he had to do was leave the equipment there and forget about it, trucks, earth-movers, cranes, compressors, barges, generators, pumps, engines, concrete-mixers, and so on. It was a fair offer, it was an offer Conrad couldn't afford to reject. Any businessman in his position would have accepted it—no questions asked on either side.'

'What are they doing with this stuff in Jarma?' Stallard asked.

She looked up at him, her eyes imploring him to believe her. 'I swear to you, Stallard, I have no idea, and neither does Conrad.'

He believed her now. She had told him all she knew, but not all her husband knew. Whatever was going on in Jarma, Stallard reckoned, Conrad Hasseler was up to his neck in it.

Then Godwin said, 'They must be using it for whatever they're doing in the Cut.'

'What?' Stallard asked.

'Hasseler's heavy equipment, in Jarma. Remember Showqi said something about some big construction job that was being done in the Cut, and nobody knew what it was.'

'I don't know anything about that,' Virginia Hasseler said. 'Please believe me!'

Stallard turned away from her. 'I believe you,' he said.

'Can I have my daughter back now, please?'

'I doubt that she'll go with you, Mrs Hasseler,' Stallard said. 'She certainly won't if you intend going back on board the yacht.'

'Why not?'

'If she went back onto the yacht, her life wouldn't be worth a farthing.'

'Don't be a fool, Stallard!' the woman said. 'Davies wouldn't dare touch her!'

'He dared touch her in Angola!' Stallard snapped. 'If it hadn't been for me and Godwin, she'd be dead *now*!'

The woman was silenced, a look of total perplexity on her face.

Godwin said to her, 'When Sigrid disappeared in Europe, and you knew that she was with Showqi, why did you inform the police?'

'We thought they were running away together to get married. We wanted to prevent that, so we informed the police, made her a ward of court, and that's how the newspapers got hold of it.'

'And you knew, of course, when she and Showqi joined the yacht at Tenerife,' Stallard said.

'Jamil told us. And as his son was wanted in Jarma, Jamil presumably also told Colonel Davies.'

'I suppose then,' Stallard said, 'that Showqi, as a fugitive from justice, wasn't murdered—he was killed resisting arrest.'

'Yes,' the woman said, 'I suppose that is what Davies will tell Jamil, anyway.'

'Well, he wasn't resisting arrest, Mrs Hasseler,' Stallard said, with anger. 'He was running, to save Sigrid from the sadist who was whipping her. And he was shot down like a dog.'

'Drink, anyone?' Godwin asked.

She served more drinks. As she handed the glass to Virginia Hasseler, the woman looked up at her and said, 'Tell me about this Mrs Black, please.'

Godwin told her of how she had come to meet Mrs Black, and the story that Mrs Black had told her. When she had finished, Virginia Hasseler sat staring straight ahead, grim-faced.

At length, the woman said, 'How can she be sure Sigrid is her daughter?'

Neither Godwin nor Stallard attempted to answer her.

Then she said, incredulously, 'All these years, she's had our servants spying on us.'

Godwin lit a cigarette.

Then, urgently, Virginia Hasseler said, 'You must never tell Sigrid any of this!'

'Neither of us will ever breathe a word of it to Sigrid,' Stallard assured her. 'I'm sorry we had to use it so—so brutally against you. But our lives are being threatened, Mrs Hasseler. Cynthia's and mine and Sigrid's, and now maybe yours too.'

'Mine?' she asked.

Stallard nodded. 'Colonel Davies isn't a lone ranger.

117

He's not running around the world killing people for no reason, he's taking orders from someone, and it has to be either Jamil Bazarki, or your husband, or possibly both of them.'

'So I have been, as you say, a bloody fool,' Virginia Hasseler said.

'I'm going to Bahrain,' Stallard said. 'You'd better come with me.'

'Why are you going to Bahrain?' Godwin asked him.

'I want to take my boat and go across to Jarma,' he said. 'I want to find out what's going on in the Cut. There's only one way I can see of getting out of this mess alive—and that's by getting to the bottom of it.'

10

Two days after leaving Cape Town, Stallard and the three women arrived in Bahrain. Although Stallard advised her that she was inviting disaster, Virginia Hasseler did not intend to miss the grand opening ceremony of the Jarma Causeway which now was only five days away. With Jamil Bazarki, she had worked hard for the causeway, and so her attitude was understandable in a way. But she also discounted Stallard's fears for her safety; she felt she knew the extent to which her husband was involved in the so-called Bee Sting Deal, and she was firmly convinced that Jamil Bazarki was not involved in it at all. She was certain that both she and Sigrid would be safe in Jarma, once Jamil had arrived on the scene.

Mrs Hasseler and Sigrid went to stay with some friends in a mansion on the beach at Budeya, and Godwin moved into Stallard's house in the date palm groves just outside Manama, the main town; and on the afternoon of the day of their arrival, Stallard drove over to Jufair to call on the Royal Navy.

The commanding officer of H.M.S. *Jufair*, was a grey-haired, red-faced man named Commander Anderson. With him in his office was a short, tough-looking American with a tight black crew-cut, who wore a suit that seemed to be made out of tinfoil. Anderson introduced him to Stallard as Mr Garfield. Stallard had had previous experience of these characters, and he knew without having to be told that Mr Garfield represented the Central Intelligence Agency.

They all sat round a table on which stood an ice-bucket, a bottle of Scotch, a bottle of gin, several tumblers, cigars and cigarettes and the rest of the appurtenances to a cosy afternoon in the air-conditioning.

Stallard sipped good Scotch, sucked on a good cigar, and told his story from the time of his arrival in London and his meeting with Jamil Bazarki and Conrad Hasseler at the Dorchester. When he had finished, Commander Anderson asked him, 'You believe you're still in danger from this Colonel Davies?'

'I'm damn sure I am,' Stallard said. 'And so are the women.'

Garfield said, 'We might be able to arrange some protection for them here. But not if they go to Jarma.'

'And you, Mr Stallard,' Anderson asked, 'do you want protection too?'

Stallard rolled his cigar between thumb and two fingers and studied it, absently. 'I came really to ask your advice,' he said. 'I was thinking of taking my boat over to Jarma and having a look into the Cut; see what the hell is going on.'

'How were you planning on getting into the Cut?' Garfield asked.

'With an aqualung, forty or fifty feet down.'

'Commander Anderson's already tried that,' Garfield said, and looked at the Navy man.

Anderson said, 'The mouth of the Cut is guarded by an MTB which carries two twelve-millimetre machine-guns.

We sent two frogmen in last week. They ran into a heavy-gauge anti-submarine net. Since then we've fully investigated that net. It's firmly bedded at the sides, and my men went down deeper than they should have done—three hundred and twenty feet—trying to find a way under. But that net goes all the way down, and the water is four hundred and fifty feet deep. There's no way round it and no way under it, and to cut through it you'd need oxy-acetylene.'

Slowly, Stallard nodded. Then he smiled. 'That's the sort of advice I wanted,' he said. 'Save me going on a wild-goose chase.'

'What were you expecting to find in the Cut, anyway?' Garfield asked him.

'A submarine,' Stallard said.

Garfield nodded.

'A damaged submarine,' Stallard said. 'Damaged about three months ago in a collision with a tanker called *Atlas Monahan*.'

Again Garfield nodded. 'In fact, there are two subs in the Cut,' he said, and quickly added, 'this is strictly within these four walls, you understand. Both are nuclear-powered and probably armed with Polaris-type missiles. They're not British and they're not American, so you can draw your own conclusions as to who owns them. The one that was hit by the *Atlas Monahan* was lucky. The collision occurred in relatively shallow water—no more than sixty fathoms—and she was hit well forrard and away from her business section. Even so, they had to damp down her pile immediately, because of the risk of a radiation leak. The other sub had to come in and get her out of there. Apparently that's not a too difficult job in shallow water where you can have divers working outside, and where the damaged sub still has power to blow her floatation tanks and give herself a bit of buoyancy—as must have been the case. They were able to tow her, submerged, into Jarma Harbour, surface her, and take her into the Cut, where the job of patching her up is now in progress.'

'Using Conrad Hasseler's equipment,' Stallard said.

120

Garfield nodded. 'They'd need to get her out of the water, so they'd have to build some kind of dry-dock.'

Stallard looked at Commander Anderson. 'The R.N. had a tender up there looking for this sub—at that time it was being called "a whale"—after the collision.'

'And we found it,' Anderson answered. 'But it was in international water, it wasn't a wreck, or a derelict—there were still live crew inside it—so we couldn't touch it. And, of course, we still can't.'

'If she'd foundered, say, within the Bahraini concession area, we could have pulled her in,' Garfield said. 'And by Christ we would have done, friend, make no mistake. The *Pueblo* incident galled.'

'And your relations with Jarma are not as amicable as they are with Bahrain,' Stallard observed.

'It's not that,' Garfield said, frankly, 'it's just that the Russians got to Jarma before we did.'

Drawing on his cigar, Stallard eyed Garfield through the swirling blue smoke. 'But not before the Persians,' he said, quietly.

Garfield bent his head forward and studied the top of the table while, assiduously, he scratched the back of his neck. 'Yes,' he said, at length. 'And that's what the Bee Sting Deal is all about, I'm thinking.'

'What do you mean?'

Garfield stood up—he was a restless little man—and thrust his hands deep into the pockets of his trousers. Turning from the table, he walked across to the window, from where he looked out onto ordered green lawns and slick black tarmacadam drives, and the square with the white mast at its centre, and the White Ensign drooping from its head in the hot, gold stillness of the day.

'We've had word,' he said, 'from one of our people in Moscow, that a guy named Severin has been sent to Jarma. This is puzzling us, Stallard, because as far as we can see, they have no need of a guy like Severin in Jarma. He's not Navy, he's not an engineer, he knows nothing about repairing damaged submarines; he's a diplomat, putting it politely.

121

Putting it bluntly, he's a professional spy. He's organised some very big deals for the Rousses in Western Europe, the States, and Japan. And as far as we can see, sending him to Jarma to supervise this job in the Cut is about like posting the captain of the English test cricket team to lead an expedition into Antarctica, if you'll excuse the implications of the instance conjured up in the heat of oratory.'

Stallard grinned. Garfield was quite a character. He turned from the window his tough, pale face still deadpan. He said, 'If Severin's behind the Bee Sting Deal, the Bee Sting Deal is not good.'

'What do you think he's up to?' Stallard asked.

'Let me tell you about this guy,' Garfield said, and picked up an attaché case off the floor by the chair he had been sitting on. From the case, he took a manila folder, opened it, and passed it to Stallard. 'That's him,' Garfield said. 'That's Bimbo Severin.'

The folder contained a ten-by-eight monochrome portrait photograph of a man. About his eyes there was an intelligent and faintly humorous look, but his mouth was lipless and somehow forbidding. His hair was pale, possibly sandy, and cropped very short around a well-formed head. The set of the square, strong jaw indicated power both of physique and will. On the left side of his throat, under the jaw-line, there was scarring, like old acne or small-pox, but it did not disfigure so much as add interest to the smoothly groomed but generally rugged features of the man. He would have been about Stallard's age, maybe a little younger, and the weather-roughened and darkened complexion could have denoted a skier, or a deep-water yachtsman, or a mountain climber.

'Handsome brute, isn't he?' Garfield said. 'And there's a brain there too. At Leningrad in 1954 he took first-class honours in politics, economics, English, and French. He was also an Olympic skier. At the age of thirty-seven he's what you might call the darling-boy of the Soviet Union, and that's why he's allowed so much freedom of movement. He's got dames in Geneva, Paris, London, Washington, and 'Frisco—and they're just the ones we know about. Every one of them would knock your eye out and every one of them is worth at least a million bucks. He plays a mean game of mixed doubles and he's a killer at the bridge table. When he's in town, every society hostess in New York is wetting her bloomers to get him at her next cocktail party.'

Garfield poured himself a gin and tonic, sipped it, then said, 'He's also pretty damn mean with a 7.65 millimetre Makarov. You see that scar tissue round his left jaw? He got one of our guys in a corner in Berlin once. Our guy squirted him with nitric acid; Bimbo just put his arm up to cover his eyes and kept on coming on, straight into a shower-bath of nitric acid, and he killed that guy with his bare hands. The plastic surgeons patched him up.'

Stallard now understood Garfield's problem.

'What the hell is a guy like that doing in Jarma?' Garfield asked.

Jarma. A few hundred square miles of barren rock and sun-blasted, sterile gravel peopled largely by nomadic Arabs, bedous, camels, goats, and a donkey or two, where the biggest society function of the week took place at the mosque at noon on Fridays; it was a society of which there were no female members at all, let alone the kind of females Bimbo Severin would be interested in. There was one hotel in Jarma town, rigidly dry and rigidly men-only. If Severin was in Jarma, he certainly wasn't there from choice.

'How long has he been there?' Stallard asked.

'According to our information, slightly more than two months.'

'He'd be getting a bit homesick by now, then,' Stallard observed.

'You can say that again.'

'You wouldn't like to do us a favour, would you, Stallard?' Anderson asked. 'I mean, as you were planning on going over to Jarma anyway . . .'

Stallard looked at him. 'What sort of a favour?'

Anderson looked at Garfield. The American said, 'We

123

want to know what's going on over there, Vic.'

'I could get killed over there,' Stallard protested.

'From what you've told us about Colonel Davies,' Garfield said, 'you could get killed anywhere.'

'What's it worth?' Stallard asked.

Garfield leaned on the table, towards Stallard. 'You come back with some intelligence, Vic,' he said, 'and you name your price. It will be paid.'

As Stallard viewed his situation now, he had little or no alternative but to go over to Jarma and try to get to the bottom of the Bee Sting Deal. It was the only way he could see of getting himself, Godwin, and the Hasseler girls, off the hook. Otherwise, this infernal cat-and-mouse game he had been playing with Colonel Davies across half the world for the past three weeks might continue indefinitely.

After leaving the Naval base, he took a few quiet drinks alone at the Gulf Hotel, and did some thinking about the situation in general and about Bimbo Severin in particular. And out of a number of slugs of Scotch and ice, a plan came to him which at first appeared ridiculous, even suicidal; but the more he thought about it, the more it appealed. At length he called the boy to bring him a phone, and he rang Anderson at H.M.S. *Jufair*.

He asked the Commander, 'Can you fix me up with a couple of phoney passports?'

'By when?' Anderson asked.

'Tomorrow morning.'

'I'll get on to the Political Agent,' Anderson said. 'Who are the passports for?'

'Me and Cynthia Godwin. I want them as if we're man and wife, I'm Fred Bloggs, she's Una Bloggs, housewife. Or something.'

'Can you get a couple of photographs around to the political agency this afternoon?'

'Yes,' Stallard said. 'Thanks.'

'And don't use "Bloggs", Stallard, please. It's my mother's maiden name.'

On the way home he bought a set of water-skis and a tow-rope and he stopped off at one of Manama's more *chic* boutiques, and bought a present for Godwin.

A messenger from the political agency delivered the passports to Stallard's house the following day at 8 a.m.

The island of Jarma lies approximately 140 miles northeast of Bahrain, on the other side of the Persian—or, as the Arabs prefer you to call it—the Arabian Gulf. The sea that morning was of that almost sensuous texture of a pale, highly polished turquoise, which you find only in shallow, tropical water. It is the ferocity of the sun bursting through the glassy surface and glowing back off the fine sand bed, white as milk. Off the coast, out of sight of land, the hue of the sea becomes a deeper, more luxuriant blue, patched with dark areas where coral or drifts of weed lie below.

There was not a cloud in the sky as Stallard's boat, the *Sandman*, put out of Manama harbour upon this beautiful sea, and her twin screws quickly wound her up to around twenty knots to cut a long, straight wake, the shaft of the spear whose head was the sinuously travelling arms of her bow-wave. In the high-chair, behind the wheel, sat Ali, Stallard's crew-man, one-eyed, dark-brown, wizened and wrinkled and hard as a dried betel nut, keeping her steady on forty-five degrees.

In the saloon below, Stallard handed over the present he had bought Godwin in Manama.

'Try it on,' he instructed her.

She unwrapped it and from the paper took a minute G-string with a matching and equally minute bra. 'Darling,' she smiled, looking delightfully surprised, 'when do I wear this?'

'This afternoon,' he said. 'You're going water-skiing in Jarma Harbour.'

Her delight turned into a kind of sick incredulity. '*What?*'

'Bait, darling.' He grinned at her. 'I'm trawling for a shark.'

'Vic, this isn't a swim-suit!'

'What is it?'

'It's a nonsense, strictly for the boudoir. It won't last five seconds on me water-skiing.'

'All to the good,' he said. 'You'll attract the shark even faster without it.'

'No!' she said, emphatically.

'Have a drink,' he said, handing her the tumbler he had just charged for her. Then he went up on deck. He told Ali to go below and prepare some food, and he took over the wheel, checking the compass heading.

A little while later, Godwin poked her head around the edge of the saloon door and looked up at him. 'Tell Ali to shut his eye,' she said.

He grinned. 'Ali's below.'

'Well,' she said, and came on up.

The effect of the G-string and the miniscule bra was electrifying. From the back she looked naked, from the front, tantalisingly, almost so. She minced down the deck as if she were on a catwalk in a Paris salon, turned expertly, and minced back. That was a thing about Godwin, she walked well, with a jauntiness and a light-footed swing. Seeing the G-string on her, however, Stallard changed his mind about using her as bait to catch Bimbo Severin.

'Maybe it is a bit much,' he conceded, 'or a bit little, as the case may be. Have you got anything else you can wear?'

'No, darling.' She smiled. 'Nothing at all.'

'Hell, honey, you can't go water-skiing in that thing.'

'I'm afraid, darling,' she smiled again, 'it's this or nothing.'

He looked away. 'Maybe nothing would be better,' he muttered.

From behind him, she put her arms round him and cooed, with her lips against the back of his neck, 'Don't you think I'll catch your shark?'

He lit a cheroot and discovered that his hands were trembling slightly. 'Yes,' he said, hoarsely. 'You'll catch him all right.'

About three o'clock in the afternoon a long, low dust-smudge was visible on the horizon dead ahead. Gradually

126

it grew and solidified into the deeply furrowed, limestone cliffs of Jarma, eroded and scoured by relentless winds.

The *Sandman* turned north, running for Jarma Heads, with the pale triangle of a dhow sail on the horizon running with her.

Beyond the northern tip of the island now a short stretch of the fabled Jarma Causeway was visible, a pale strip of concrete on the blue water, curving to disappear over the horizon. Just below the northern point, on a natural table of rock about halfway up the cliff face, stood Jamil Bazarki's palace. Stallard had seen the place before, from the sea. It was an incredible place, an enormous, rambling house built entirely of white marble, surrounded by Acropolean pillars and terraces gleaming like snow in the sun, high above the sea, against that sun-scorched, dun-coloured, sterile cliff. The entrance to the harbour was about a mile south of the house.

The harbour is the only good thing about Jarma. The only natural deep-water anchorage in all of the Persian Gulf, it is locked on all sides by two-hundred-foot cliffs that plunge, below sea-level, between another three- and five-hundred feet to the bottom. The harbour is a bowl about two miles in diameter, whose sides, of crumbling limestone have been shredded over aeons by infrequent but torrential downpours of rain, creating gulleys and rifts that narrow and rise as they run away inland. In one of these valleys, and about the sides of the hills enclosing it, the town of Jarma stands, an unprepossessing place and, because of its siting, brutally hot. Many minarets tower above rising terraces of flat roofs; the buildings are all uniformly square and uniformly white, and the town collectively resembles a handful of toy blocks dropped by an infant giant upon the hillsides, that have slid and tumbled down into the valley floor, or been caught on rocky snags and left straggling about forlornly along the lower slopes.

The Europeans who came here to build the Jarma Causeway were the first Westerners who had ever had to spend any time here; at first the company sent them to Beirut

127

for a month after every three months on station, but by the time the job was nearing completion, the Europeans had to go to Beirut at the end of every month. That was not one of the 'perks' of the job, it was fully paid leave and wholly necessary to save the men from going out of their minds.

As you enter Jarma Heads and move up the narrow neck, called the Khorr-Adjra, that leads into the harbour, the opening called the Cut is bearing about thirty-five degrees to you. The Cut is not an erosion valley, like the rest of the clefts indenting the harbour walls, but a gigantic split in the earth's crust made by a 'quake a million years ago. Thus it is said that the Cut is bottomless and the water in it goes on down into the very pit of Hades, and in olden days persons convicted of capital crimes were executed by being thrown into the Cut.

The only other object of interest in the harbour is Bazarki's wharf, on the seaward side in the north-west corner, below the ridge on the other side of which stands Bazarki's marble palace. But Stallard was not concerning himself with Bazarki's wharf as the *Sandman*, at half speed, moved out of the Khorr-Adjra across the lake-still waters of the harbour; he was focussing a pair of binoculars on the mouth of the Cut, away to the south.

It was like a section taken out of the Grand Canyon of the Colorado and scaled down by a factor of about three. The top quarter of the eastern cliff face was bathed in molten gold by the sun which was now well past its zenith. The rest of the cliffs over there, and the still waters below them, lay in deep, silent shadow, and across the mouth of the Cut was moored the old motor torpedo boat with its twelve-millimetre machine-guns mounted fore and aft. It was battleship grey, an ex-First World War German Navy boat, and Stallard wondered where they'd brought it from and what sort of speed it would do. It looked big, fast, and uncomfortable, and it also looked deserted.

The whole of the vast harbour, in fact, looked deserted. He swept the glasses around the cliffs to the wharves below the town where one ship was moored, a rust-streaked, black

128

steamer of some seven thousand tons, flying the Liberian flag. Moored alongside her was a big barge, but on neither the ship nor the barge nor the wharf was there any sign of life. The ship was probably the sub tender Showqi Bazarki had mentioned. Continuing his sweep, he found no vestige of life anywhere.

At the north-western corner of the harbour there was another wharf, surmounted by a great sign in English under Arabic, proclaiming the area to be the property of Jamil bin Sharif Al Bazarki, to be Strictly Private, and to be kept out of. It was a long, stone dock with some stone and corrugated asbestos sheds at the back of it, against the cliff face. From one end of the dock, a gravel road joined it to the town several miles away around the edge of the harbour, and from the other end a flight of stone steps led up the mountainside and over the top, and, presumably, down the other side to that white palace above the sea.

A torpor lay upon this great, hot bowl half full of tepid water, a sense of dullness and stupidity and sleep, as though the very air were exhausted.

He lowered the glasses and looked down at Godwin.

She lay on a towel on the upholstered bench seat in the stern wearing a black straw hat and sun-glasses and that minute black G-string and bra. Her body glistened, and the deep tan she had acquired during the week on the *Shaheen*, ending in expanses of milk-white skin, vividly measured the difference in size between the bikini she had worn then and the outfit she wore now.

'Get your skis on,' Stallard said. 'Let's wake this graveyard up.'

The *Sandman* was not an ideal water-ski boat. She had the speed, but she was far too big to have the necessary manœuvrability. In the vast, empty harbour, however, no pinpoint turns or dead stops would be required of her, and by being careful Stallard reckoned he could get away with it. The launch hove-to and Godwin went over the side into the blood-warm sea. He passed the skis down to her, then he lowered the bar of the tow-rope and she gripped it, look-

129

ing up at him and laughing. 'I've lost it,' she said.

'Lost what?'

'The bloody G-string!'

'Don't mess around, woman, please!' he pleaded.

'Well, hang on, the string's come undone at the side.' She spent some more time with her head under the water. When she surfaced, she said, 'Okay. For the time being.'

'You *can* do this, I hope?' he said to her.

'Do what?'

'Water-ski!'

'Try me,' she said.

He signalled Ali, at the wheel, to go slow while he kept a light strain on the tow-rope. It went out thirty feet before it sprang taut and she began moving, low in the water, her arms out stiffly, parallel, ahead of her, and her knees up under her chin. Stallard went forrard and took over the wheel and, looking astern, eased the throttle levers out. The *Sandman*'s engine-note rose and she surged ahead, bows rising, digging her transom down into the furrow of her wake. The tow-rope rose horizontally from the sea, springing and tight and flinging off droplets of spray all along its length. Godwin came up to stand on the skis, slightly bent at the knees, riding on the now bucking water. The G-string, he observed with relief, was still where it should be; she was laughing and she held the tow-bar with one hand and waved to him with the other. He eased the accelerators further forward, opening the boat right out, and swung her into a long, speeding curve.

The roar of the engines rang across the still water to the cliffs and rolled back in long, soft-echoing waves. Her wake was a white sickle-blade lying flat on the blue surface. Down the middle, it was a trench of bursting foam enclosed by sliding banks of water and Godwin, as if she'd been born on water-skis, swung back and forth across it, over the lip of one bank and down and across the boiling trench and up the other bank and out widely curving across smooth water and back again. Expertly, her legs absorbed the shocks of meeting each trough of disturbed water and

130

needles of spray lanced her flesh as she burst through walls of dead air.

On his second circuit of the harbour, Stallard steered further south, wheeling round to roar close by the big MTB at the mouth of the Cut. Two men in drab grey uniforms stood in the well-deck, one leaning on the gunn'le, as the *Sandman* whipped past them. The big, grey boat was rocking in the launch's wash as Godwin passed it, waving to the men, who, laughing, waved back at her.

Godwin, however, attracted no sharks, either of the aquatic or the anthropoid varieties, and Stallard eventually had to consult his chart of the harbour to find a spot shallow enough to anchor. He found such a place at the northern end, and on the seaward side, about two hundred yards off Bazarki's wharf. He reeled Godwin in, and while she was having a shower he poured some drinks.

'No luck?' she called from behind the plastic shower curtain.

'Give it time,' he told her. 'It will probably take an hour or two for the word to circulate. You can't expect your shark to be lying under the boat with its mouth open, waiting for you to drop your hook.'

Then Ali called from on deck. 'Sahib Vic, boat come.'

He went on deck. A small, high-prowed Arab dinghy was approaching from the direction of the town, propelled by what sounded like a crudely converted diesel truck engine mounted inboard. There were two people aboard, an Arab in a white *thowb* and skull-cap, and another Arab in official-looking khakis and a black and green peaked cap. He wore a gun-belt and a holster, both highly polished, as were his black boots and his incongruous brown leggings.

The bloody Law, Stallard thought.

The dinghy drew alongside and the policeman grabbed the rail of the launch. 'I am Sergeant Noori,' he said, 'Jarma Customs and Immigration Department. May I come aboard?'

Stallard reached down to him and helped him aboard. He showed the sergeant his and Godwin's passports, which named him and Godwin as Mr and Mrs Roberts, of London.

'Nobody else aboard?' the policeman asked.

'Only the crewman. Ali.'

'Why have you come to Jarma?'

Stallard shrugged, smiling affably. 'We had a couple of days to kill in Bahrain, so we thought we'd hire a boat and have a look around the Gulf. We had heard of your beautiful harbour here and were passing by, so we thought we'd drop in.'

'You don't have visas for Jarma.'

'We weren't planning on going ashore.'

'You've hired the boat?'

'That's right.'

'May I see the boat's papers, please.'

Damn you, Stallard thought. He went to the locker in the bulkhead ahead of the wheel and took out the *Sandman*'s registration, ownership, and insurance papers. The policeman examined them at length, laboriously copying details from them into his note-book. Then he handed the papers back.

'The owner is Victor Stallard, of Manama,' he observed.

Stallard shrugged. 'I don't really know who the owner is. My agents handled the hire for me.'

The Arab nodded. 'Okay, Mr Roberts. How long you be staying?'

'Probably until tomorrow. We'd just like to put up for the night here, if that's okay?'

'That's okay. You can go ashore if you want to, but you must obey any notices you may see, particularly about restricted areas. They are in Arabic and English both.'

'Fine,' Stallard said. 'Thank you.'

The sergeant went back over the side into his dinghy, and his crew boy pushed off and headed across the water towards the town. The sergeant stood in the stern waving a nonchalant farewell to the *Sandman*.

It would take the Russians about four generations, Stallard reckoned, to drill any kind of respect for official and recognised procedures into these indolent, casual, and rather likeable people of Jarma.

Godwin came on deck, her short hair still wet and slicked back around her head. She wore a loose, white dress, just hip-long and supported solely by narrow tapes over the shoulders, which offset the glowing satin sheen of her suntan. 'I attracted the wrong shark,' she said.

'I have been a bloody fool,' Stallard told her.

'What exactly brought the fact home to you?' she asked.

'I fixed us up with fancy phoney passports and forgot about the boat's papers.'

'But you said you'd hired it.'

'Colonel Davies is that copper's boss,' Stallard pointed out. 'Davies is not going to swallow that there's a Mr and Mrs Roberts in the harbour on a boat owned by Victor Stallard.'

She shrugged. 'How do you know Davies is even here? He's probably still lying face down in Luanda with his arse *bien cuit* aimed at the ceiling fan.'

Stallard laughed. 'It's an attractive prospect,' he said. 'But I don't hold out much hope for it.'

'Well then?'

'Well then, what?'

'What do we do? Get out?'

'No,' he said. 'Not yet.'

'What then?' She looked across the water, darkening now as the sun went down. 'The bright lights of Jarma?'

'Let's see what's in the larder,' he said. 'I'm goddam hungry.' He called Ali up. 'Ali,' he said. 'Is that steak thawed?'

'Yes, sahib, all ready.'

'What else is there?'

'Prawn, sahib. Smoke salmon, avocados, onion, mash powder, ketchup, bake beans, spaghetti, smoke ham . . .'

'Steak and smoked salmon,' Stallard said. 'Serve it about eight. And the wine, on the gimbal shelf in the liquor cabinet, okay? Chateauneuf du Pape.'

133

'*Eenam!*' Ali said, with enthusiasm, for when Stallard feasted, so did Ali.

'And remember the Prophet!' Stallard called after him, as the little man disappeared in the direction of the galley. Ali, in gastronomical fervours, sometimes neglected the word of the Koran for the sake of taking a glass of burgundy with his curry.

Laughing, Godwin came across the deck and put her arms around Stallard's neck. 'I love you, you great oaf,' she whispered.

His arms went round her slender body and held her against him and he kissed her cheek-bone and her hair and whispered against her ear, 'I love you too, skinny.'

The sun had sunk behind the cliffs now and the deep blue shadow of the great harbour wall crept across the water towards the still sunlit land. A blessed coolness descended, and with it the world seemed to come back to life. White gulls sailed down across the water, or floated on fat feathers, casting for fish. Away on the dust-shrouded roads of the island an occasional ray of the dying sun bounced off the windscreen of a car in a blinding explosion of white light, and the sounds of the town came intermittently, ringing across the water like scraps of paper in a breeze, a muted snarl from an exhaust, a horn honking, a donkey's bray, a dog's bark, a cock's crow, a mild cacophony overlaying a continuous, intrusive, high-pitched wail, the mullahs from the minarets issuing the call to evening prayer.

Stallard and Godwin dressed for dinner, which was to be served by Ali on deck. The Arab had set up a folding table with two chairs there, and linen and cutlery and all the accoutrements were beautifully arrayed. With the innumerable diamond point stars that scatter themselves across the Arabian sky at night above them, they dined by the glow of the *Sandman*'s rigging lights and the light from the saloon, spraying out, with music from the hi-fi, through the open door into the cockpit.

Halfway through the meal, Stallard signalled Godwin to be quiet.

134

'We've got company,' he said softly.

She listened, and heard oars timidly lapping in the dark water beyond the rail. There was a gentle thud against the launch's transom, and then silence for a moment, just the noises from across the water in the still, hot night. And then the boat rocked, suddenly and violently so that Godwin had to grab the wine bottles on the table to stop them falling over, and there were scuffling and bumping sounds from the stern, and then there he was—in full evening dress, crouching on the transom grinning widely and wildly at them, with a mist-beaded silver ice-bucket, containing three bottles of Bollinger champagne, lovingly tucked under either arm. The shark had risen to the bait. 'May I join you?' he asked.

'Come right in,' Stallard told him.

Bimbo Severin, lithe as a tiger, stepped down off the transom onto the deck planking of the *Sandman*.

Stallard called towards the open door of the saloon: 'Ali! Bring up another chair.'

11

Severin was a man of charm. His grooming, despite that he had already spent two months in almost monastic seclusion on this desert island, was immaculate, and his manners faultless.

At the end of the meal, as they sat in the warm night with brandy and coffee, the Russian said to Stallard, 'Mr Roberts, that was an excellent meal. Thank you.' He looked at Godwin and smiled, 'And thank you, madame.'

She smiled back at him.

'Pardon me if I tend to stare at you,' Severin said to her, 'it is a long time since I've seen a woman, and even longer since I have seen one as lovely as you.'

135

'You may stare all you like, Mr Severin,' Godwin said. 'I'll just sit here and be shy and confused and ladylike.'

'You were water-skiing,' Severin sipped his brandy, 'quite naked, I am told.'

'Not quite naked. Just almost.'

'It's as well I missed it,' the Russian said, 'it would only have unsettled me.' He looked at Stallard and laughed.

'What are you doing here, Mr Severin?' Stallard asked.

'Well,' Severin said, and sighed deeply. 'I am swimming, I am sunbathing. I am skin-diving, I am spear-fishing, I am boozing, I am playing chess, I am sleeping. In that order. That is my undeviating programme for every day of the week, every week of the month, and if, when I get out of this place, I ever see another fish, or another chess-board, I swear I will blow my brains out.'

'When are you getting out?' Stallard asked.

'At the end of this week, I fervently pray. Oh, there is to be a grand party the night before I go. They are coming, the rich and the famous of Europe and America, here to this miserable heap of gravel in the middle of the sea, for the most glittering and star-spangled social occasion in the history of Jarma—the celebration of the opening of the Jarma Causeway. Have you seen the causeway yet?'

'We saw just a bit of it as we were approaching the island,' Stallard said.

'You saw the white house on the cliff over there?'

'Yes, I saw the white house,' Stallard said.

'That's where I'm staying. You will be my guests there tomorrow, please. And then we will go and see the causeway properly and maybe Mrs Roberts will water-ski, yes? No? Anyway, this causeway, it is a magnificent thing, a road across the sea to blue Persia far away, forty kilometres long, a monument to man's ability to reshape his environment.'

'You're here in connection with the causeway then?' Godwin asked.

'I'm here for my sins,' Severin smiled at her. 'Or perhaps my indiscretions. My superiors, and presumably, bet-

136

ters, felt I was having too fine a time on the Cote d'Azur, so they sent me out here to dry out. But I am going to laugh last, my friends. When I get out of here I am going to write my memoirs; it will be a best-seller and make me a millionaire. I'm going to call it *400 Kilometres Up*. You know why? Because this Persian Gulf is the rectum of the universe, and Jarma is four-hundred kilometres up it.'

Godwin laughed.

'Tell us more about this great celebration,' Stallard said, lighting a cheroot.

Severin said, 'The main party, next Friday night, will be held up at the house where I'm staying now. The house is owned by this man Bazarki, whose name you see on the wharf over there, and who practically owns Jarma. Bazarki built the causeway, he is a millionaire many times over. At the moment, I understand, he is aboard his yacht heading this way with a number of his more illustrious guests. I heard he is even importing the Bluebell Girls from Paris for this party. Now look, why don't you both hang around for that? Come to the party as my guests, it's only three or four days from now, you have the time surely?'

'That's very kind of you,' Stallard said. 'It sounds tempting.'

'It isn't very kind of me.' Severin grinned. 'You know how all these Arabs are, with their *citron pressé*, and these Bluebell Girls I hear are all virgins; I would like to be assured that there are at least two hard drinkers at this function besides myself.'

'And one non-virgin,' Godwin said, smiling icily.

Severin laughed. 'But they are the most interesting women, Cynthia!'

They talked and drank until about 4 a.m., when the Russian took his leave, climbing with remarkable agility for a man with at least a bottle of brandy and two of champagne inside him, back over the transom and into his dinghy. He paddled off into the darkness shouting his farewells across the harbour at Godwin and Stallard, who had promised to breakfast with him up at Bazarki's house.

137

For all the talk, however, Stallard had learned nothing of interest from Severin that night, and for some time after going to bed he lay awake, smoking and thinking. Severin was a cunning Russian, and there was no way Stallard could see of trapping him, tricking him, or inveigling him into saying anything he did not want to say. Stallard concluded that the only thing he could do for the moment was stick around and keep his wits about him. He could only hope that somewhere along the line an exploitable situation would arise, or somebody would drop an unguarded word which might mean something.

In the event, it was the cunning Russian who dropped the unguarded phrase; but he did it deliberately.

On the following afternoon, Stallard and Godwin, both suffering fierce hangovers, climbed the long steps up the cliff face from Bazarki's wharf, under a terrible sun, and stopped at the top to recover, light a cigarette, and contemplate the cosmos. To the north lay the Jarma Causeway, a narrow, black and white ribbon stretched tightly across the shallow, milky turquoise sea to disappear into the distant, dun-pink dust haze, which was Persia. Behind, to the south-east, and immediately below, was Jarma Harbour out of which they had just climbed. The *Sandman* floated way down there like a white toy on the water which was so crystal clear that the boat's shadow was visible on the white sand of the harbour bed fifty feet further down. To the west, the Gulf reached out deep blue to the horizon; and just a little way down the cliff ahead of them stood the palace of Jamil Bazarki. If Stallard had not already formed suspicions about Bazarki's integrity and decency, the sight of the house the man lived in would have aroused them.

Looking down on it, even through the dark lenses of his sun-glasses, he was dazzled by the blaze of the sun off almost two acres of Pentellic marble. A sprawling terrace surrounded the house and a swimming pool of Olympic proportions. Tables and chairs were shaded by lurid sun umbrellas; a fountain played skyward from the bell of a trumpet blown by a giant, naked, white marble Diana the

138

Huntress, who was also armed with a mighty bow and attended by a brace of slinking hounds upon a pedestal at the centre of a lily-pond; trees and shrubs grew out of broad, white urns filled with imported black earth, and vines and creepers climbed and writhed and curled around the tall Doric columns and over the arches and swarmed across the white-faced walls. It was the sort of house Caligula would live in.

At the far edge of the lowest of the terrace levels was a long, low wall of marble pedestals surmounted by blocks, and beyond this wall a sheer, hundred-foot drop to the sea.

Stallard and Godwin went on down, to breakfast.

During the next few days they swam, played tennis, swam, did a lot of drinking and talking, swam some more, and ate, all in the company of Bimbo Severin, but learned nothing about him they did not already know, except perhaps that he was a pretty good swimmer. For periods on each day, he left them and was gone they knew not where for a couple of hours. He explained these absences from the scene with a shrug and by saying, 'I have to do something to justify my existence.'

On Thursday, the guests started arriving, the people who had been invited to Jarma for the causeway opening ceremony and the great social gala that was to follow it. In the morning two plane-loads came in, and in the afternoon boats began cluttering up the harbour. Mostly they were small, about the dimensions of the forty-three foot, twenty-three ton *Sandman*, but a couple were large and rather luxurious, more in the class of Bazarki's *Shaheen*—which, of course, had not as yet appeared. These big yachts brought the local shaikhs and their entourages from Jarma's big, oil-rich brothers around the Gulf, and their companies, as did the companies of most of the other boats in the harbour, remained aboard. The people who had come in by plane, Stallard learned from Severin, were being accommodated at Bazarki's palace, but in a different wing from the one the Russian was occupying. For this, Severin was grateful, as he did not wish to have to associate with these

139

people. This surprised Stallard, as the Russian had done a great deal of complaining about the loneliness he had endured over the past two months. The reason became obvious that evening.

Stallard and Godwin were dining with Severin at the house. They arrived and were announced by the Indian butler and Severin was awaiting them in a room off the lobby. It was a large and magnificent room, as were all the other rooms in this magnificent house, with a great Tabriz carpet on the floor. It was furnished with enormous and sumptuous leather couches, its white marble walls decorated with intricated Arab silver and a fine collection of antique eastern rifles. One end of the room was open, the ceiling there supported by four tapering pillars beyond which was the vast, deep indigo night dusted with stars. Severin stood with his back to the room, leaning against one of the pillars and looking out at the sky. Over his shoulder, then, the Russian dropped that unguarded word:

'Come in, Mr Stallard.'

Throughout the week he had known Stallard and Godwin as Frank and Cynthia Roberts.

As he said this now, he turned to them. His right hand was in the pocket of his evening dress trousers, the other held a highball glass.

Stallard stared straight back at him, considering his situation.

Then, breaking the sudden tension, Godwin crossed to the liquor cabinet and began pouring herself a drink. 'How long have you known, Bimbo?' she asked.

The Russian shrugged. 'Ever since you first arrived in the harbour.'

Then he smiled very briefly at Godwin, without his eyes ever losing sight of Stallard. 'I was told to expect Mr Victor Stallard; I was told all about him, and about you, my lovely Cynthia, but I did not in my wildest dreams expect him to bring you with him.'

'Why, then, the charade?' Stallard asked, sombrely. 'Calling me Frank-ole-boy, and all that.'

'I apologise for that,' Severin said. 'It was unforgivable. But I just did not want to ruin it. I've enjoyed the past few days immensely.' He grinned, and then looked at Godwin. 'Are you pouring the drinks, my darling?'

'The usual?' she asked them both.

When they had their drinks, Stallard sat on one of the big couches and Godwin remained standing by the liquor cabinet. Severin lounged with one hip on the arm of another couch, facing Stallard. 'Why did you come here, Vic?'

'The main reason,' Stallard said, 'is this fellow Colonel Davies. He's chased me halfway around the world over the past few weeks, trying to kill me. I wanted to find out why.'

'You mean you don't know?'

'I'm damned if I do,' Stallard said.

'You don't know about the Bee Sting Deal?'

'I've heard the words spoken. I don't know what they mean, I don't know who are the parties to the Bee Sting Deal, or what it involves. I know nothing at all about it, Bimbo.'

'It is considered that merely to have heard the words spoken is enough to get you killed,' Severin said. 'I had to kill a man in New York for no better reason.'

Stallard looked up at him.

Godwin said, softly, 'Schreiber!'

Severin nodded.

Stallard breathed deeply, perplexed. 'But what is so fatal about these three words, Bimbo? They mean nothing to me, they meant nothing to Showqi Bazarki, or to the man Schreiber; they meant less than nothing to this journalist in London who was murdered by Davies. It seems pointless, senseless, to me.'

Severin said, 'The problem resolves itself into two halves of a jigsaw. The knowledge that you have, that Miss Godwin has, that the now dead ones had, that presumably by now the two Hasseler women and this other woman in London, this Mrs Black, the knowledge that you all have, is

141

one half of the puzzle. You know a little more than nothing about it, Vic. You know that it involves blowing up the Jarma Causeway. Charles Schreiber figured that out—he arrived at his conclusion *via* the wrong avenue, he thought that Conrad Hasseler was going to blow up the causeway to conceal his poor workmanship—that is not the reason; but the causeway *is* going to be blown up. The knowledge you people have, then, is one half of the jigsaw. When the bridge is destroyed tomorrow night, and if you are allowed to witness the events which follow, you'll have the other half, the picture will be an intelligible whole to you, and the knowledge you have, then, will become compromising. So all of you, I fear, must die.'

Stallard sat in silence, watching the man.

Severin was, for the first time since their acquaintance began, grave. He said, 'I, thank God, am not to be your executioner.'

'Who is?' Stallard asked. 'Davies?'

Severin remained silent, just watching Stallard.

'Is he here now?' Stallard asked.

'He arrives tomorrow,' the Russian said. 'With Bazarki and some other guests.'

'What makes you think,' Stallard said, 'that I'm going to hang around until tomorrow?'

'You've no alternative, my friend,' Severin said, lifting himself off the arm of the couch and commencing, introspectively, to pace the carpet. 'The MTB you have no doubt observed which is moored at the mouth of the Cut, has orders not to let you out of the harbour. Even if you beat her out, she can outrun you—I'm sorry, a warship is not a "she", is it?—but those torpedo tubes along the MTB's sides are not merely decorative. There's a real live, armed, primed, and fused torpedo in each of them. She'll catch you up and blow you sky high.' The Russian stopped pacing, turned, and looked directly at Stallard. 'I would genuinely like to get both of you off this hook you're on; but I can't. Particularly you, Stallard. You are more dangerous, a greater threat to the success of the Bee Sting Deal, than the rest of them put together.'

'Why?' Godwin asked.

'Stallard has had the opportunity of knowing more about it than the rest of you,' Severin said.

'If I've had such an opportunity,' Stallard said, 'I've missed it.'

'The yacht,' Severin said, 'is the Bee Sting.'

'What does that mean?' Stallard asked, genuinely puzzled.

'You sailed in her for over two weeks. You had the opportunity to observe that there was certain equipment aboard her.'

'Then I didn't observe it,' Stallard said.

'You probably did, Victor, but it didn't register. When I explain to you what the codewords Bee Sting stand for, it will register—something you have noticed, unconsciously, unseeingly at the time will suddenly assume importance, and you will remember it. That's what I mean by two halves of a jigsaw.' Severin looked at Godwin. 'Another drink, Cynthia? Sit down, please, let me get them.'

Godwin came and sat on the couch with Stallard who now was deep in thought. He did remember—a short, hollow, metal pillar on top of the wheel-house on the *Shaheen*, with a bunch of disconnected electric cable sprouting from the end of it. Andreas had explained it away as a post for a new radar antenna. It was, however, a strange-looking post for a radar antenna, and for a while Stallard had wondered about it; but in the heat of what had happened in Angola, it had gone completely out of his mind.

As he poured the drinks, Severin said, 'Tomorrow, at 2 p.m., there is to be a great function. The official, ceremonial inauguration of the Jarma Causeway. At his end, the Prime Minister of Persia will sever a silk tape with a pair of twenty-two carat gold scissors, and at this end the Ruler of Jarma will do likewise. The two dignitaries, followed by their entourages, will then drive to the centre of the causeway, meet, shake hands, and mouth a number

143

of fatuous words. They might even waste a bottle of perfectly good champagne. At this juncture it had been planned to destroy the causeway, and commit the Prime Minister of Persia, the Ruler of Jarma, and all their attendant dignitaries to the whim of the wind—this, mind you, was Bazarki's plan; it had nothing to do with the Soviet Union.' The Russian was smiling at Stallard as he carried the drinks over. 'You, Victor, thwarted that plan, with a little help from Miss Godwin.'

'Unintentionally, I assure you,' Stallard said.

'Perhaps,' Severin agreed. 'You see, to blow up the causeway, we had to have the yacht here. The necessary equipment is aboard her—that is why she was at Hamburg, to have this equipment installed. The opening of the causeway was brought forward, and so, to make sure the yacht was here on time, Jamil Bazarki retained you, Vic. Without any knowledge of the Bee Sting Deal, and what it involved —without, that is, one half of the jigsaw—anything strange you may have seen aboard the yacht could have been explained; even when the causeway was blown, it was felt, you would not have connected the explosion with anything you had seen on the *Shaheen*; without that first half of the jigsaw, the second half would have been meaningless to you. But as soon as it was known that you were aboard the yacht and in possession of that first half of the jigsaw—you had to be disposed of.

'You know, of course,' the Russian went on, 'that there is explosive sealed into the pylons of the causeway. The only way in which this explosive can be detonated is by a radio signal. The receiving aerials for the signal are camouflaged within the lamp-posts on the causeway and only two people on earth know what the signal is, and the frequency and wave-length at which it should be transmitted. One is a high Persian civil servant, the other is Jamil Bazarki. So, in theory, Bazarki could blow the causeway without the equipment which is installed in his yacht. All he would need is a moderately powerful transmitter, such as you have aboard the *Sandman*. But that would give him away—it would inevitably become obvious to a commission of inquiry that Jamil had done the deed. The deed, therefore, has to be done more subtly. Hence the equipment on the yacht.'

Severin sipped his drink. He was standing in the centre of the room, watching Godwin and Stallard intently. 'You've heard of a MASER,' he said. 'Microwave amplification by stimulated emission of radiation. It can be used, in one form of its development, to concentrate electromagnetic waves within the visible spectrum into a beam of light that will punch a hole in armour plate. Then it is called a LASER. The Bee Sting apparatus is a further development of the principle upon which the MASER and the LASER are based— it will amplify, by stimulated emission of radiation, electromagnetic waves of very great wave-length, in other words, radio waves. Bee Sting, of course, is not the code-name under which research into this phenomenon is being undertaken in the West. Otherwise your friend Garfield, in Bahrain, would have realised immediately what was going on. I presume you spoke to Garfield in Bahrain?'

Stallard nodded. 'He has the first half of your jigsaw too. And by now, so does CIA headquarters in Virginia.'

With a touch of melancholy, Severin smiled. 'The CIA can't touch Jamil Bazarki. Not while he's under the wing of the USSR.'

'Carry on,' Godwin said to the Russian, 'the Bee Sting apparatus...'

'Well,' Severin said, 'the tactical importance of the Bee Sting is best illustrated by the line being followed by researchers in Russia at the moment. They're working on a missile armed with a Bee Sting head, which will draw its power from a nuclear pile no bigger than a football. From orbit fifteen hundred kilometres up, this missile in a split second, could deactivate every receiver of electromagnetic waves in the Western hemisphere. It would blot out all radio, television, and of course radar, communication. The Bee Sting homes on a transistor or a valve, overloads it and kills it. It only needs a power source. The apparatus on the yacht is an early Bee Sting, primitive but powerful enough for Bazarki's purpose. From a range of about five kilometres, using the yacht's own generators as a power source, he will be able to kill the tiny receivers in the bases of the causeway pylons, and thus detonate the explosive. After the explosion, it will appear to have been an accident. The most thorough investigation will reveal no evidence of anything other than failure on the part of the detonating mechanism.'

Stallard looked at Godwin, who sat at the other end of the settee from him. Then he looked back at Severin. 'What was aboard the yacht that I should have seen and didn't?' he asked.

'If you had gone into the radio shack you would have seen the firing mechanism. Also, above the bridge housing, you could have observed a short, stainless steel pillar with a cluster of disconnected power cable sticking out of the top of it; the Bee Sting radiator barrel fits to the top of that pillar?'

The Englishman nodded. Of course, he realised, what Severin said was true. With his suspicions already aroused, with the knowledge of the situation he already possessed, once the Bee Sting Deal was put into operation and things started happening, Stallard would be able to fit the pieces of the jigsaw together—and then he would be dangerous.

'Why,' Godwin asked, 'should Jamil Bazarki, who has worked practically all his life for this causeway, now that it's finally been built, want to blow it up?'

'The causeway that has been built,' Severin said, 'is not the one for which Jamil has worked all his life. You heard what the American said on the tape recording. What he said is true. The causeway is a complete travesty of every principal of construction engineering. It is a pale parody, a sick caricature of the great structure Bazarki had always envisaged, and far from being the everlasting monument to his name which he sought to erect, the Jarma Causeway probably won't even outlive him. We, the Soviet Union—for our own reasons, admittedly—have offered him the

146

chance to try again, and do it properly, and do it with his own money, with capital raised in an economically viable, independent state of Jarma, on his own terms—not, as things are at the moment, on terms dictated from Teheran.'

'And in return for this big investment,' Stallard asked, 'what are you, the Soviet Union, going to get out of Jarma?'

Severin shrugged. 'We have our reasons,' he said, enigmatically.

'A submarine base?' Stallard suggested.

'You *have* spoken to Garfield,' the Russian smiled. 'Haven't you? So I suppose you know what's going on in the Cut. We have a submarine in there, badly damaged. They've been working on her for three months now, trying to patch her up well enough to be able to run submerged for Odessa. Had it not been for the proximity of this harbour here, at Jarma, when that sub was hit by the tanker, we'd have had no alternative but to have left her where she lay, on the sea-bed. We could not have even got her as far as Fao; she was falling apart when we got her in here as it was. If we had had to leave her on the sea-bed, the Americans would have salvaged her—with ninety per cent of her crew still alive inside her. You can imagine the embarrassment that would have caused the Soviet Government—a *Pueblo* incident with the boot on the other foot, so to speak. The incident put the cap on the argument, sealed the decision—if we were going to be a military force in this part of the world, we had to have a base here. Jarma is absolutely perfect for our purposes. From one carrier in this harbour we can cover the Middle East from the air. From here, our subs can cover the Indian Ocean, the Southern Ocean, and the South Atlantic.'

'And, of course,' Stallard said, 'Persia. If you own Jarma, you've got Persia surrounded.'

The Russian smiled, but said nothing.

'So you were going to blow up the bridge,' Stallard said. 'As you've guessed, I spoke to Mr Garfield in Bahrain. The fact that the Persians might prove an embarrassment to Soviet aspirations here, arose then. You wanted the

Ruler of Jarma and the Prime Minister of Persia on the causeway when it went up—to instigate temporary political vacuums in Teheran and here, and make the takeover of Jarma so much simpler—followed, possibly, by the takeover of Persia. No?'

The Russian just shrugged and turned away. 'Well, we can't get the two leaders on the bridge now, so that plan has had to be rethunk.'

'Sorry I let you down,' Stallard said, with irony.

Severin looked around and grinned at him.

Stallard got to his feet and paced, deep in thought, upon the Tabriz carpet. At length he asked the Russian, 'How do you feel about it personally? I mean about Cynthia and me having to be eliminated.'

Severin said, softly, avoiding Stallard's gaze, 'It's necessary.'

'For the good of mankind?' Stallard asked.

'Have another drink,' Severin said, and collected their empty glasses and went over to the liquor cabinet.

'What about the other people who have what you call the first half of the jigsaw?' Godwin asked. 'The people we've spoken to, the people Showqi spoke to before he was killed . . .'

'People you've spoken to,' Severin said, 'are not important. Hearsay isn't evidence. And Conrad Hasseler can keep his wife and daughter quiet.'

'So Hasseler is involved,' Stallard said.

'He has allowed us to use his company's equipment to build a dry-dock in the Cut. He has accepted money from the Russian Embassy in London.'

'What about Garfield?' Stallard asked.

'What can he do?' Severin countered. 'He can make a report to his superiors. His superiors can make reports to the President of the United States; but Jarma is not Cuba. They are not going to go to war over Jarma.'

'They might over Persia.'

'If they do, my friend,' the Russian said, gravely, 'you won't be here to see it. The only person other than yourselves who concerns us in any way now is this woman, Mrs Black, whom Davies could not get to in London. She concerns us primarily because we just don't know what her interest is or how she came by the knowledge she seems to have. It was she who involved you two, so possibly now there is something you can explain to me.'

'Her interest isn't political,' Godwin said. 'It's purely personal.'

'Elucidate,' Severin said.

'She's Sigrid Hasseler's mother,' Godwin said, and told the Russian all about Mrs Black.

When she had finished, Severin nodded thoughtfully. 'I see,' he said.

'She doesn't give a damn about the balance of power in the Middle East, Bimbo,' Godwin said. 'So long as Sigrid is safe she's no danger to you whatever.'

For some moments, Severin considered this assurance. Then he said, 'Well, we shall see.' He turned towards Stallard who was now standing with his back to the room, at the far end, between two of the massive marble columns, looking out across the dark sea into the ink-blue depths of the night. 'Shall we dine now?' Severin asked.

'For some reason,' Stallard said, without turning, 'I just don't feel very hungry any more.'

'Damn!' Severin said. 'I knew this would happen. I really did not want to ruin our last night.' He looked pathetically at Godwin, miserable as a boy deprived of a Christmas present. 'I really didn't,' he told her, sincerely.

12

On their arrival back at the boat that night, Stallard and Godwin found Ali in a state of near hysterics. During Stallard's absence, the *Sandman* had been visited by some people from Jarma, radio technicians, who, despite Ali's protests, had taken the transmitter apart and put it back together again so that it did not work.

Throughout the remaining hours of darkness, Stallard had paced the deck and Godwin had sat on the rail watching him, as he tried to find an avenue of escape for them. But it was hopeless; to get the boat out of the harbour he would have to pass within a hundred yards of the MTB, whose crew must surely spot him and stop him. He thought about trying to escape across the causeway, by going into Jarma town and stealing a car; but there was a customs barrier at each end of the bridge, and the guards on those barriers would certainly have been alerted to the fact that Stallard and Godwin were carrying phoney passports, not to mention the problem of papers for a stolen car.

They were trapped.

In the morning, a helicopter came across the island from the south where the landing-strip was that Jarma called an airport. The 'copter cleared the northern escarpment and sank behind it, presumably to land on one of the broad, white marble terraces of Bazarki's house.

From the *Sandman* in the harbour, Stallard and Godwin heard, rather than saw, the opening ceremony of the causeway from the north, beyond the high cliffs above Bazarki's wharf. There was much muffled drumming and thumping, and the ragged tear of a twenty-one-gun salute being fired over there just after 2 p.m. Then, the more important guests were ferried back to Bazarki's house for the commencement of the festivities. They came in convoys of Cadillacs and Lincolns and Grand Mercedes, roaring around the harbour road and raising great fog-banks of yellow dust, to disgorge their passengers onto the wharf. There they entered the long, corrugated-iron building above which Bazarki had erected his great sign and from where a funicular railway, which ran in a shaft sunk almost perpendicularly through the cliff, took them up to the house.

In the middle of the afternoon, Severin came down to the wharf, got into the dinghy he used, and rowed out to the *Sandman*. He climbed aboard and stood on the deck in the burning sun wearing crisp, white slacks and a blue towelling singlet. On his feet he wore rubber flip-flops and on his head just a pair of black, wraparound sun-glasses. Stallard was lounging disconsolately in the high arm chair behind the wheel, sucking on a can of beer. Slowly, he pushed the swivel chair around so that he faced the Russian.

'Can you spare one?' Severin asked him.

'One what?'

'A beer. I'm goddam thirsty.'

'You know where it is,' Stallard said.

Severin went on down into the saloon, to the refrigerated liquor compartment under the hi-fi console, and supplied himself with a can of beer. As he was tearing the cap off the can, Godwin came through from the cabin. 'Come up,' Severin said to her, nodding towards the cockpit where Stallard was. 'I want to talk to you.'

Godwin was wearing just a yellow, towelling bath-robe. She walked across the saloon and up the four steps into the well-deck and sat down on the upholstered lid of the locker along the starboard side. Severin leaned in the open doorway, looking up at them.

He drew on the beer can, then fastidiously wiped the froth off his upper lip on the back of his left wrist. 'Why don't you come up to the house?' he said. 'Everybody's up there, we're having a few drinks.'

Stallard said, 'Is this it, then?'

'Look,' Severin said, 'forget what I said last night, will you? Maybe it's not going to happen.'

'You're kidding,' Stallard said, with sarcasm. 'You wouldn't kid us, would you, Bimbo?'

The Russian hung his head, grinding his teeth together, fiery with anger. 'Come on up,' he said quietly. 'Jamil wants to talk to you.'

'So this *is* it,' Godwin said. She lingered a moment, then went below and put on a cotton dress and sandals and Severin rowed them ashore in the dinghy. They climbed

151

the long stair in the sun, up the cliff face, and from the top of the ridge looked down on the great, white, marble house just below. On the terraces, groups of people stood about talking and drinking. They were mostly lightly and informally clad, some in swim-suits, and the pool was being well patronised. On the broad area beyond the pool, a big helicopter was parked, its rotors drooping. Rosaries of as yet unlit coloured light-bulbs were strung on black cable between the potted shrubs and the Doric columns and the walls of the house. A wreath of genuine olive leaves was wilting about the white stone head of Diana the Huntress, and the chatter and talk and tinkling, cackling laughter wafted dully upwards in the still heat. Severin led Stallard and Godwin down and into the party.

They were supplied with drinks, and the host came over to greet them. He wore Arab dress, and he bowed, after the fashion of Arabs, to Stallard. 'Hallo, Vic.' He smiled. 'So glad you could come.'

Stallard smiled. 'Nice of you to invite us,' he said.

The Arab turned to Godwin. 'We haven't met, Miss Godwin. I'm Jamil Bazarki. Welcome.'

'I've met your son, Mr Bazarki,' Godwin said, coldly.

If the barb hit home, Bazarki did not show it. He looked back at Stallard, still smiling. 'You've been very clever, Vic. For a while there, until you showed up here, I thought you might have beaten me. Why did you walk straight into it?'

'Being too damn clever, I suppose,' Stallard said.

'You made a mistake in trying to outwit Bimbo Severin, my friend. He is a professional intriguer.'

'So I've learned,' Stallard said.

Godwin was looking around her, at the other guests talking, strolling with their drinks in the hot sun, hearing shrill shrieks and great splashes from the direction of the swimming pool. How could she communicate, how could she get through to them, and make them aware of her and Stallard's situation?

Then, with a group not far off, she recognised Virginia

152

Hasseler. The fools, she thought, why didn't they stay in Bahrain—Sigrid was there too. And then, in misery, Godwin thought, why didn't we all stay in Bahrain?

Bimbo had rejoined them, having been off talking to some women.

'Bluebell Girls?' Godwin asked him.

'No.' He grinned. 'Casino du Liban.'

'Are they virgins?'

He shrugged. 'We shall see.'

'When's it going to happen, Jamil?' Stallard asked the Arab.

'When is what going to happen?' Bazarki appeared puzzled.

'The execution,' Stallard said.

'I really don't know what you're talking about, Victor,' Bazarki said, glancing quickly at the Russian and looking pained.

Severin stepped in front of Stallard and eased him away from Godwin and Bazarki, whispering, 'Come with me.' When they were apart from the others, Bimbo went on, quietly, and in deadly earnest: 'There's a gun on your head right now,' Vic. Don't force them to do it here.'

'Why not?' Stallard asked. 'Because it will make a mess on the patio?'

'If you play your cards right, Victor, I might be able to get you out of this alive. Don't spoil it.'

Stallard's eyes became that pale, ice blue they assumed when his gut was full of hate; he spoke softly, unhurriedly, but meaning it: 'Don't do me any favours, Bimbo. I'm not dead yet, and when I go I just might take a few of you bastards with me.'

Severin would have laughed at that, but for what he saw in the other man's eyes; what he saw, had he been a lesser man, would have frightened him. As it was, for the first time since meeting Stallard, Bimbo understood why Colonel Davies had put this Englishman top of his death list.

At length, Stallard turned and left Severin; he walked away across the patio alone among the happily chattering

153

guests; they were like figures in an exhibition; the cacophony of their prattle, the clink of ice-cubes on glass, the
shuttling and bowing of waiters, in the boiling, blinding
blaze of the sun on the white marble, it was all a stage set,
a scene played and replayed and now stale and meaningless with its endlessly repeated rehearsal. They were department store dummies, and as Stallard strolled among
them, one of the dummies reached out and grabbed his
arm, looking up, smiling, into his face.

It was Sigrid Hasseler, but he could not bring himself
to acknowledge her, he felt himself so far apart, so alien,
among the dummies.

He stood at the edge of the terrace, his drink on the low
stone wall there, gazing straight down at the ripe green sea
a hundred feet below. The sea was littered with boats, like
feathers dropped by seagulls. The people in the boats had
come to see the causeway opened and now were waiting for
the night when the vast black sky and its unnumbered stars
would form the back-drop to Bazarki's pyrotechnics display, and the mellow darkness would be cut and blasted
and ripped asunder by the thunder and lightning of a million sizzling lights and bursts of white fire and monsoon
rains of glittering sparks.

Small boats, big boats, sail and power boats, exotic and
humble boats, there must have been five hundred visible
from where Stallard now stood, and for a time he brooded
on them. Then he sensed the presence of the Russian just
behind him.

Softly, Severin said, 'I can at least get Godwin off the
hook.'

'Do that then,' Stallard said, without turning around.

Sigrid Hasseler was standing by his left elbow. 'What's
the matter with you?' she asked.

He looked down at her. 'You seem remarkably happy,'
he said, 'for a young lady accepting the hospitality of the
man who murdered her lover.'

She scowled. 'No, Vic,' she said, shaking her head with
absolute conviction. 'Jamil is not involved.'

154

'His own son,' Stallard went on. 'The bastard murdered his son.'

'No!' the girl declared.

Her mother came over, smiling at Stallard, extending her right hand. 'Hallo, Vic,' she was saying.

Stallard ignored her hand. 'Where's Davies?' he asked her.

'How do I know?' the woman said. 'He's not here.'

Stallard was not looking at her, but looking around the groups of guests on the terrace. 'He is, you know,' he said, and his eyes had fixed on a man on the other side of the patio. The man was glimpsed only briefly, as groups and individuals moved around, now obscuring, now revealing him; but the man himself did not move. He was a slightly built, heavily-browed fellow in a sharply cut brown tropical weight suit and a white shirt open at the throat. That was the gun Severin had warned Stallard was on him. To Virginia Hasseler, he repeated, 'Davies is here.'

'Well, I certainly haven't seen him.'

'Where's your husband?' Stallard asked her.

'He's over there.' She nodded in the appropriate direction.

Hasseler was there, elegant and cool-looking as usual, in white pigskin casuals, slacks, and dark, tight-fitting shirt; he was sipping iced lager and chatting with some other, equally elegant people.

'You must have been insane to come here!' Stallard whispered, with a trace of anger, at the woman.

'You've still got this thing about Jamil, haven't you?' she said.

Over her shoulder he could see Bazarki coming across the terrace, excusing himself, smiling, as he brushed past people, towards Stallard and Severin and the Hasseler girls.

'Yes,' Stallard said. 'I've still got it. And pretty soon now, you're going to have it as well.'

Bazarki joined them. A little way behind him, Godwin stood. 'Come with me,' the Arab said.

'Where to?' Sigrid Hasseler asked.

155

'Inside. I want to talk with you.' He looked up at Stallard. 'All of you.'

'What if I don't want to talk with you?' Stallard asked.

'You wanted to know when it's going to happen, didn't you?' Bazarki said. 'If you come with me now, you'll find out.'

'And if I don't go with you, it will happen now,' Stallard said.

'Exactly,' Bazarki said, then turned and led off.

The women followed him, and Stallard followed the women.

Sigrid Hasseler looked round at Stallard. 'When what's going to happen?'

He remained silent, his face grim, his eyes hidden by the wraparound sun-glasses. Behind him came Severin and Godwin, and behind them, Conrad Hasseler was coming along as well. They crossed the terrace and went up three shallow steps onto a patio; from there, they passed under a great arch, into the house.

From each side of the hall a broad, shallow-stepped staircase curved gracefully as a swan's neck up and around the walls to the floor above. Even with that huge archway open to the day, the silent, concealed air-conditioning cooled the immense volume of the place. Bazarki mounted the stair to the right, and they followed him. At the top, they were in another hall, long and broad, white and cool, with a great door of carved ebony leading off each side. The Arab opened the door on the seaward side and silently invited them to pass through.

In the opposite wall of the room they now entered were two huge french windows in fancy, wrought-iron frames. Vines and leaves of wrought iron were worked and welded into the glazing of these windows so that when they were shut and locked, as they were now, they were as effective as the bars in the casement of a jail. There were three men already in the room. Two stood at one end and were Jarmani policemen, wearing the regulation stiff khaki shirts and shorts, heavy black boots with brown leather leggings, black and green peaked caps, highly polished shoulder-straps and gun-belts; and each of them held a machine pistol in his right hand.

The third man stood with his back to the room, gazing out of one of the french windows, across a broad, tiled verandah shaded by a high, arched roof, down onto the terrace where the party was going on. Farther out, beyond the edge of the terrace, was the sea with those hundreds of scrap-like boats scattered about its emerald surface. The man at the french window was short and thickset and broad. He wore a fawn suit of ultra-lightweight cotton weave, above which his bulldog neck bulged flaming red. Spiky, snow-white hair, like dry, wind-blown grass, grew around the sides of the head, and that flame-red flesh glowed again across the top of the bald scalp. He stood with his feet apart, his hands clasped lightly behind his back, and in one of them he held a thick, heavy-looking bamboo cane. Seeing it, Godwin gasped, and Stallard glanced quickly at her.

Behind them, the great ebony door swung silently to.

Jamil Bazarki stood in the centre of the room and said, 'Ladies and gentlemen. For the benefit of those of you who have not as yet made his acquaintance, this is Colonel John Davies, Chief of the Jarma State Police.'

The man at the french window turned to face into the room. Stallard had looked at him through the scope sight of a rifle in Angola, but this was the first chance he had had of making a close scrutiny of Colonel Davies. The man's eyes, he observed, were hooded; thick pads of flesh dropped almost to cover the irises, hanging lower at the outer corners, so that there was an opaqueness about the gaze, a peculiarly insensitive and immobile quality, like the gaze of a reptile, or a bird. Without seeming to move at all, the eyes took in the group and each individual member of it. Then they fixed on Stallard.

Davies smiled. 'Mr Stallard,' he said. 'We meet at last. I shall carry the scars of our previous encounter to my grave.'

'For which, I hope,' Stallard took a cheroot out of his shirt pocket, 'you don't have very long to wait.'

Davies laughed. 'I'm sure you do,' he said, and then the merriment froze. 'But my grave is further from me than yours is from you, my friend.' Then he looked at Godwin and smiled again. 'We meet again, Miss Godwin.' To Virginia Hasseler, gallantly, he bowed. 'Virginia.'

Lighting his cheroot, Stallard looked down at Virginia Hasseler. A look of dawning horror was creeping across her face. 'Believe me now?' he asked her.

'Jamil,' she said, pointing at Davies, 'this is the man who killed Showqi.'

'I know,' Bazarki said, gazing flatly back at her.

Sigrid Hasseler screamed: 'No! No!' and then she added, softly and with sudden fear, staring at Bazarki: 'You murdered your own son.'

Conrad Hasseler gripped the girl's arms and interrupted her: 'Jamil, do you mind if I take my wife and daughter out of here while you attend to . . .'

'Yes,' Bazarki snapped, 'I do mind, Conrad. We have to decide here and now what is to be done. Who is to remain here and who is to leave. Concerning Miss Godwin and Mr Stallard, there can be no argument. They stay. You, Conrad, I can trust, because you are a clever man and you stand to lose a great deal by saying the wrong things in the wrong quarters. But of your wife I have doubts; and of your daughter, I fear, grave doubts.'

'I'll vouch for them, Jamil,' Hasseler said, grimly, almost desperately. 'I swear neither of them will talk, Jamil!'

Suddenly, Sigrid Hasseler went mad, in tears, screaming and cursing at Jamil Bazarki. Her father held her back. The girl was hysterical, and Godwin stepped in front of her and slapped her face, twice, back and forth with her right hand. The girl sagged, her father taking her weight, sobbing pitifully.

Watching her, Bazarki said quietly, 'I understand your

158

concern, Conrad, but your assurances are just not strong enough protection for me.'

'Bazarki,' Stallard said, 'the girl knows nothing. Let her go.'

'She knows too much!' Bazarki said. 'She has already seen too much here in this room.' Then he turned to Davies. 'I know, John, how dearly you would like to handle this situation yourself, in your own way, especially in the case of Mr Stallard. I am sorry, but I must deprive you of that gratification, or satisfaction, or whatever you would derive from it. It has to be done my way, do you understand?'

The hooded eyes moved imperceptibly to focus the Arab. There was a quality of mutiny in the air about the Colonel.

'You must do it my way, John!' Bazarki insisted. 'You must understand, the amount of money that has been spent on the Bee Sting apparatus has not been mere extravagance —it has been essential, to make the destruction of the causeway appear, under the most minute and thorough of investigations, accidental. After the explosion there are going to be inquisitors here from all over the world, possibly even the U.N., probing and questioning, and we simply cannot afford to have unnatural deaths occur at this time, other than those that are going to occur inevitably, when the bridge blows up. These people here must be alive and on the bridge tonight, with the roisterers and revellers, when the explosion is detonated.'

Davies' eyes moved back to Stallard, and the man remained silent.

Bazarki continued: 'The C.I.A. man in Bahrain, the British too, know that Stallard and Miss Godwin are here. This is why I allowed them to be seen at the party downstairs this morning—it can be shown afterwards that they were my guests here and, unfortunately, among the victims of this regrettable accident which is going to befall the so-called Jarma Causeway. It must be this way, John, we have come this far and we simply cannot afford to take any chances now.'

Slowly and, it seemed, grudgingly, Davies nodded. Then

159

he said, 'I shall probably have to give them each a hit on the head to keep them in position on the causeway, you understand?'

'Of course,' Bazarki said, matter-of-factly. 'From what is left of them after the blast, nobody will be able to tell that they were hit on the head before it.'

Then, for the first time since they had entered this room, Bimbo Severin spoke. He was standing to one side of Stallard, Godwin, and the Hasselers, and he said to Bazarki, 'I would like to enter a plea on behalf of Miss Godwin.'

'What do you mean?' Bazarki asked him.

'Cynthia,' Severin said, and she looked around at him. His face deadpan, his mouth hard and tight, he said, 'Marry me, and come back to Russia with me.'

Godwin was awestruck. She gaped, open-mouthed, at the Russian.

Beside her, Stallard said quietly, but with urgency, 'That's a fair offer. Accept it.'

Godwin felt weak in the knees and her head spun; she could not comprehend what Severin had said to her. Stallard gripped her about the waist and she held his arm. Then she was bawling and sobbing and she blurted out: 'No. Thank you, Bimbo, but no.'

'You bloody fool!' Stallard whispered, still holding her, and to the Russian he said, 'Come and take her. Come on, man!'

'I can't take her against her will, Vic,' Severin said.

'Go with him,' Stallard told her, 'for God's sake, go with him.'

She just shook her head, sobbing against his chest.

After a moment, watching her, Bazarki said, 'That, it would appear, is that.' Then he looked at Severin. 'Very noble of you, however, Bimbo.' He smiled.

Severin's lips curled as if he had a mouthful of rotten fish, and he cast a murderous glance at the Arab.

The black look seemed to disturb Bazarki, who was obviously made to realise that he had spoken out of turn; but the upset was quickly passing. 'Well,' Bazarki said then, and looked around at Davies, 'I shall leave this matter in your capable hands, John.' He then turned to the small group of condemned people, and smiled expansively, like a man who has competently carried out a weighty duty. He said to them, 'Now I must say farewell. We shall not meet again, in this life, so for the benefit of Mr Stallard, who wanted to know when it was going to happen I shall tell you now. About sunset, Mr Hasseler and I shall fly south in the helicopter which will put us aboard my yacht, *Shaheen*, somewhere to the north of Qishm. *Shaheen*'s estimated time of arrival within Bee Sting range of the causeway antennae, is 23.45 hours local time. That's when it's going to happen, Mr. Stallard, at a quarter of an hour before midnight.'

Sigrid Hasseler had stopped crying. She stood, held loosely in Virginia Hasseler's arms, her face wet with tears, but her jaw set tightly and her eyes cold with hate, watching the Arab. Bazarki walked across to them, meaning to address Virginia Hasseler, and the girl tore herself from the woman and attacked him, spitting, screaming, kicking, lashing at his eyes with her fingernails, a tiger-cat gone berserk. While Conrad and Virginia Hasseler grabbed the girl, Bazarki staggered back, a hand covering a fingernail slash on his cheek, his Arab headdress torn awry on his head.

Regaining his composure, Bazarki said to Hasseler, abruptly, 'Come on!'

The man stood there, stupidly, his arms around his wife and the girl who, to all intents, was his daughter, his only child. 'Jamil,' he said, forcing his voice thickly through a constriction in his gullet, 'Jamil, I beg of you, she is mad now, crazy, she doesn't know what she's doing; but I can control her, Jamil, I swear to you I can!'

'Are you coming, Conrad?' Bazarki said, with menace, 'or are you staying?'

'Virginia,' Conrad Hasseler pleaded with his wife, 'Virginia, please . . .'

161

She did not look at him. 'I'm staying with Sigrid,' she said, softly.

The man looked around, his eyes red, pouring tears, at Bazarki.

Stallard watched, sickened but fascinated, conscious that he was witnessing the destruction of a man.

'Virginia . . .' Hasseler whispered, in utter despair.

'You go, Conrad,' she told him.

Broken, he went. There was silence for some time in the room after Bazarki and Hasseler had left it. Virginia Hasseler remained standing with her arms around the girl, their faces hidden. Godwin watched them, and, over by the french window, in sombre silence, Davies watched them all.

Stallard looked around, at the policemen with their machine-pistols, and then at Bimbo Severin. 'How did you get into this nest of snakes, anyway?' he asked the Russian.

'Politics,' Severin said as though the word were poison on his tongue, 'makes strange bedfellows.'

13

The first rocket went up just after 8 p.m., tracing a long, glittering arc across the night and then bursting in a white flash of brilliance that showered the shimmering sea far below with a downpour of dancing sparks. In the flash, the sea was illuminated as if by lightning, and as more followed the first, spiralling and wheeling and bursting across the stars, the sea and all the boats upon it down there were lit by almost continuous, flickering white light.

From the terrace of Bazarki's house, music floated up through the closed french windows of the room where Stallard and the others had spent the afternoon and, up till now, the evening. At the sound of the music, Stallard went to the window and looked down and saw that an orchestra was arranged and playing at one end, and there were couples dancing on the clear space before it. Further back, where the drinks had been served to all the merry party guests earlier in the day, tables were set out, at which some of the guests, more formally attired now, seemed to be just polishing off dinner.

By now, the helicopter carrying Bazarki and Conrad Hasseler would probably be hovering above the *Shaheen* a hundred miles south, lowering the two men to the deck.

All afternoon the problem of how to get out of this mess had occupied Stallard, but the situation looked grim. All he could do was hope. There was a gun aboard the *Sandman*, a weapon of the type with which Bimbo Severin was familiar, a nine-millimetre Makarov automatic. Stallard had acquired it years ago from a Russian journalist in Kuwait, and he kept it ostensibly for killing gaffed sharks before swinging them inboard. If the men who had gone out to the boat to ruin his radio had missed it, the gun was in the locker under the seat of the settee in the saloon. To get him to the causeway, they would have to take him up and over the ridge again, and down onto Bazarki's wharf. His hope, and a miserable one it was, was on the wharf to be given a chance, for something to distract his captors for just a second, to allow him time to get into the harbour and start swimming.

The *Sandman* was two hundred yards off the wharf, and even if he did manage to get into the sea without stopping a burst from one of those machine-pistols, he would then have to get to the boat before Davies or Bimbo did; but once aboard and in possession of the Makarov, he would be able to make life difficult for those two difficult men.

The hope, of course, was fantastic; it was really no hope at all; but it was the only thing Stallard could think of.

During the afternoon, he had had one short, terse conversation with Davies, when he had asked the Colonel: 'How were things in Luanda when you left?'

163

'I meant to ask you,' Davies answered, 'how you managed to get out of Angola when I had alerted all the border posts to stop you. But now the question becomes purely academic, does it not?'

That meant that Davies had not bothered the Voltzes, a mercy for which Stallard was grateful. Now he stood at the french window sipping a whisky and ice and smoking a cigarette. He had smoked all the cheroots he had brought with him.

Out in the sky, above the silver sea, the fantastic fireworks display continued. On the terrace, the guests danced happily and the orchestra played. From a great distance a regular pulse-beat throbbed through the hot night, like the thudding of a great drum, and with it came fitful snatches of far-off, high-pitched wailing, like many children crying together on the other side of the cliffs.

Hearing it, Bimbo Severin said, 'The natives are goddam restless tonight.' He had been out for a couple of hours and had just returned to the room.

'What is it?' Stallard asked him.

'The locals,' Severin said. 'Thousands of them, on the causeway, with drums and tambourines, and those double-bass things they play, all singing and screaming and yelling, you never saw anything like it.'

Looking at him, Stallard said, 'On the causeway? Are you going to clear them off before you . . .'

Severin said nothing, staring straight back at him. Stallard turned back to the french window, realising that his question had been somewhat naive—it was supposed to be an accident, so it would look strange if they were to clear the bridge before it accidentally exploded.

The Russian came and stood at the window beside him, looking out across the verandah at the fireworks and the sea and the boats, and the dancers on the terrace below.

Down on the water, a new shape had appeared among the boats already at anchor there, long and heavy-fronted and sinister as a shark in a school of bass. It was the MTB that had been guarding the mouth of the Cut and prevent-

164

ing Stallard's exit with the *Sandman* from Jarma Harbour. The fireworks had drawn them out—they would not have been able to see much of the display from within the high-walled bowl of the harbour; but the MTB's appearance down there put a little new heart into Stallard. They had left the harbour heads unguarded; so if he could just get to the *Sandman* and get her out, into open sea in darkness now, at night, the MTB's superior speed would not necessarily be an advantage. There were a thousand coves and bays and inlets along this coast in which he could lie up and they would never find him.

Reflected in the glass of the window, he could see most of the room behind him. At one end, on a big leather settee, Mrs and Miss Hasseler lay in each other's arms; they might have been asleep. In an arm chair facing them across a broad coffee-table, Godwin sat, quietly smoking about her thousandth cigarette and drinking perhaps her forty-ninth vodka of the day. At the other end stood the two policemen —not the same two as during the afternoon, the guard had been changed about dusk—still armed with those ugly machine-pistols which Stallard feared, and one of which, when he got down to the wharf and made his dash for the water, would probably kill him. The policemen themselves were not a particularly bright-looking brace, but armed as they were they did not need to be bright. A burst from a machine-pistol is almost guaranteed to hit everything within a ninety-degree arc either side of its original line of aim. Up and down the middle of the room, Davies paced like a caged leopard, hands behind his back, the heavy swagger-stick which was his trade-mark, swinging loosely from one hand. Like Severin, he had not been in the room throughout the afternoon; but he had been in more often than out, and on no occasion as yet had Stallard seen him sit down. The burns on what the Colonel euphemistically described as his 'back' must still have been troubling him.

The evening wore on and at nine o'clock the music from the terrace stopped. Stallard was still standing at the french window; looking down, he saw the guests who had been dancing returning in pairs to their tables, and a man in a fancy, silver-brocaded tuxedo was standing in the middle of the dance-floor addressing the company.

Severin, who was now standing at the next french window along from Stallard, said, 'The show is about to begin.'

'Why don't you go down and watch it?' Stallard asked him. That would get one of them off his back anyway— even without a machine-pistol, Bimbo Severin, Stallard reckoned, was every bit as dangerous as one of those Arabs with one.

But the Russian merely shrugged. 'There's another show later,' he said.

'Well, what about if we go down for the first house?' Stallard asked, with sarcasm. 'I don't think we'll make the second.'

Severin looked at him for a moment. Then, surprisingly, he said, 'Yes, why not?'

'Think you can arrange it?' Stallard asked him.

'I think it will be all right,' the Russian said. 'But, Vic . . .' from his hip-pocket he produced a gun—a small 7.65 Makarov, 'don't do anything foolhardy down there, huh?' From another pocket he took a short, fat silencer which he began fixing to the muzzle of the gun. 'If you try anything, I can kill you without even interrupting the orchestra.'

Stallard considered the gun, and the silencer, and then nodded at Severin, and gave him a rueful grin. He walked across to Godwin's chair. She, and Virginia Hasseler, looked up at him dully, and he smiled at them and said, 'Come on, girls, we're going to see the show.'

'What show?' Virginia Hasseler asked.

'Downstairs, the floor-show.' He looked back down the long room. Under the great, brilliant chandelier in the centre, Severin was talking to Davies. Davies did not look pleased, but eventually he shrugged and walked towards the door. As he was going out, Stallard called to him, 'Get us a good table, Colonel. Ringside.'

Severin came over and looked down at the women. 'You coming?' he asked them.

166

Staggering a little, and slightly glassy-eyed, Godwin got to her feet. 'Sure I'm coming,' she said.

Stallard helped the Hasseler girls up. The woman asked, 'Can we straighten our hair first?'

The Russian beckoned to the two policemen to come over. 'You two look after the women,' he told them. 'I will look after the man. Okay?'

The policemen nodded.

His right hand in his trousers pocket, gripping the Mak, Severin walked beside Stallard out of the room and into the hall. The women followed, with the policemen behind them.

Severin said to Stallard, quietly, 'These Arabs with machine-guns make me nervous.'

'Me too,' Stallard said.

Davies had a table ready for them on the terrace. It was, as Stallard had requested, a ringside table, but set apart from the other tables so that the closest of the other guests to it were about twenty feet away. From this table they would see the show from the side, rather than the front. Stallard, Severin, and the three women sat. The two policemen stood behind them, against the balustraded edge of the terrace, out of the light, but close enough to intervene effectively should they be required to. Davies, too, remained standing, to Stallard's left as he sat side-on to the table with Bimbo Severin seated behind him. Stallard was thus pretty well surrounded.

A waiter brought them what they ordered while the opening extravaganza burst upon the terrace before them, a troupe of bejewelled, befeathered, and bare-breasted girls high-kicking and prancing around the white marble in the blaze of white and coloured spots aimed from the first-floor verandah.

Stallard once caught Davies looking at his watch; Stallard's own watch said ten o'clock.

'How long have we got, Colonel?' Stallard asked.

Davies did not answer him. In the thrown-back spray of the spots, the leading edges of the Colonel's normally

167

florid face showed blue-white and glistened with sweat in the humidity of the night.

The orchestra blared and thundered as the girls leapt and kicked and their bosoms bounced in concert. When it was finished, they filed off at a smart trot, and the next act came on, two men with a girl who wore just a sequinned G-string. The men juggled with the girl, tossing her between them, over their heads, between their legs, and balancing her on the soles of their feet and bouncing her up and down.

The waiter brought more drinks. Stallard got another cigarette alight and looked at his watch. 10.12.

The juggling act with the girl ended in a long roll of drums and a fanfare of bugles; one of the men leapt to stand on his partner's shoulders, and then the girl was agilely hoisted to the top, to stand on the shoulders of the uppermost man, right up high against the black sky, posing coquettishly with her arms above her head. She was so high up that she could have leapt from the man's shoulders onto the first-floor verandah—or, if they had toppled in the other direction, she would have gone over the edge of the terrace and into that hundred-foot drop to the sea. The effort was greeted by a mild wash of applause from the nebulous agglomeration of heads in the darkness beyond the spotlit area.

The M.C. in the silver brocaded tuxedo returned, prancing and preening himself, and announced the next act as if it were the second coming of Christ—'The star of the Casino du Liban—Ma'moiselle de Monaco!'

Ma'moiselle was beefy and a little long in the tooth, but she sang well in the style of Piaf, *chansons* of unrequieted *amour*, finishing with a rousing rendition, in which the audience joined with clapping and tramping of feet to the strong and rollicking beat of *Milord*.

10.20. The *Shaheen* was now less than fifty miles south.

The dancing girls chased Ma'moiselle de Monaco offstage. They had changed their costumes for minute, gipsy-type outfits and the orchestra changed its beat to resemble that of a flamenco dance. The girls whirled and swung, kicking and leaping, heels clattering on the marble, in the hot, still air.

10.30. Stallard's palms were sweating, the tee-shirt he wore clung to his wet body; he lit another cigarette.

The music now was the barely audible, whining, staccato thudding of the opening bars of Ravel's *Bolero*. The M.C. was back onstage. He announced: '*La Diablesse!*' and the lights went out.

Stallard tensed, ready to spring, but relaxed almost immediately. The muzzle of the silencer on Severin's Makarov was pressed into the small of his back.

In the darkness, the only sound was of the orchestra and the rising, dropping whine building louder against its stuttering bass, climbing cruelly higher and louder, of the *Bolero*.

Beyond the terrace, above the sea, the fireworks flared and flashed, and the wailing and the thumping of the crowd on the causeway wafted across the cliff-tops.

The spotlights blazed alive revealing an imposing figure covered almost entirely by a black velvet cloak standing in the centre of the clear marble floor. As the beat thudded harder and the brass came in screaming to pick away at the insistently repeating refrain, La Diablesse stood motionless for moments. Then, barely perceptibly, the cloak moved and parted down one side, and a long, white, naked leg emerged, the toe pointed, the foot in a high-heeled, glimmering crimson slipper, the toe moving out across the white marble and the length of the woman's figure swaying now, ever so gently, with the heavily galloping rhythm of Ravel.

10.35.

Soon, from the far end of the terrace, the yacht's navigation lights would be visible in the distance.

An arm came out of the black cloak on the same side as the leg. It was a long, pale, beautiful arm, and the hand gripped a knife.

Davies was looking at his watch, then he looked down at Severin, but Severin was watching La Diablesse.

Suddenly, her left arm, across which the cloak was draped and which had been raised to cover her face, was flung out and she pirouetted so that the cloak rose wide around her, circling, and then was thrown from her. Under it she wore a scarlet satin dress, slit one side to the hip and fastened over the shoulders by narrow thongs which she slashed at and cut with the knife, moving rapidly and violently now, the music coming up like the approach of charging cavalry, a swirling, flying, flicking cascade of midnight black hair about her head, light exploding off the blade of the knife, the dress cut loose at the shoulders falling away to the waist and revealing her breasts and her back as she moved.

10.40, and Davies, Stallard could see, was getting anxious.

The strident, thundering music, fed into amplifiers and issuing through four tremendous speakers, was now of such volume that the marble slabs of the terrace trembled under its onslaught, and sweat flew from the woman's white body as she circled and dipped and curved, the heels of her slippers rattling on the floor in murderous quick time with the machine-gun beat. She was hacking now with the knife at the scarlet dress hanging about her hips, slashing at it, shredding it, tearing it from her body with viciousness and hatred in the knife, and the muscle corded and whipped under the soft, shining white skin in the fierce light.

The *Bolero* reached its zenith, a brain-crunching avalanche of thunderous sound, and hung there, a buffalo stampede on a tin roof, banging and shuddering, the juggernaut grinding to a halt, and all La Diablesse wore now was a red G-string. The knife was poised ready to slash the thongs of the G-string. When that happened, and she stood naked there on the last tremendous downbeat of the music, Stallard knew the lights would go out again, but Severin had anticipated it too—the muzzle of the Makarov was again caressing Stallard's spine.

As the ultimate, great thunderclap exploded across the

170

terrace, the G-string dropped, and La Diablesse stood purely white against the pure deep darkness of the night.

Then the terrace was plunged into a darkness and silence as absolute as if the earth had swallowed it, as the lights and the echoing amplifiers were cut simultaneously.

There was no sound at all. The flashing and hissing of the pyrotechnics in the sky out over the sea were like visions in a dream.

Against his body, in the utter blackness, Colonel Davies felt the woman pressed, her hot, naked skin beslimed with sweat; the point of the knife was against his throat and in that instant he knew the terminal shock ...

Suddenly Stallard was aware that something, he knew not what, was happening in the darkness beside him. There was a sound there, almost inaudible, a bruising of the silence, then a louder sound, a sharply sucked-in breath, and then a stupid, grunting, half-strangled scream.

A second later, the lights came up again. The stage area was deserted. On the marble beside where Stallard and Severin sat, Colonel Davies lay on his back with his mouth open, frozen in a soundless howl of terror and agony. The hilt and butt of the knife La Diablesse had used on her clothing projected from the Colonel's gullet, and the blade had gone right up inside his skull and probably pierced his brain. From the severed jugular, blood spouted black in the artificial light, into a broadening pool on the white marble.

Stallard saw the corpse and looked back at Severin, and Severin in his shock was just a split second later than Stallard who came around off his chair and whose fist hit the side of Severin's head like a sledge-hammer all in one vicious, desperate, express motion. Then Stallard was gone, leaping out across the empty stage area and diving for the cover of the tables and the startled guests who sat at them. One of the policemen, in the heat of the moment, loosed a wild burst from his machine-pistol, and then there was screaming and rising and tables upending, and, suddenly, panic. They were running, falling flat, crawling, yelling and

171

crying; and, keeping low to the terrace, Stallard was going through them rapidly, using shoulders and elbows and once or twice fists to force his passage.

He came to the edge of the terrace and the low parapet with the long drop to the sea beyond, and he took a short, low run at the parapet, vaulted it, and went over, below him nothing for an awful long way and then the sea rushing up to meet him.

Feet first, he hit the water with a crash and a shock that almost knocked the wind out of him, and then quickly folded double as he went down to arrest his rush into the depths. He got his shoes off and his shirt, and then commenced to swim, the frog-stroke underwater, heading seaward. How far out had the MTB been? A quarter of a mile? Perhaps a little more, and almost on a direct compass-bearing of 270 degrees from the house. His watch told him it was 10.55. The *Shaheen* now would have been less than thirty miles south.

The pockets of his jeans, filled with water, were like tiny sea-anchors as he swam, so he stripped the jeans off and continued in his shorts. He passed under the stern of a small Arab craft full of boys seemingly mesmerised by the fireworks in the sky; none of them noticed the swimmer, and Stallard hoped the crew of the torpedo boat would be likewise transported.

On the swim he passed several boats, but no member of any of their companies saw him, or if they did they took no notice of him. This once-in-a-lifetime display in the sky occupied every man, woman, and child of them to the exclusion of all other phenomena.

Now he could see it lying long and low on the water, broadside-on to him less than fifty yards ahead. It was in silhouette, looking bulky, but having an air of enormous, dormant power in its heavy-shouldered fore-parts, tapering away towards the waist and tail. The severity of its lines was not softened by the blank, oblong outline of the near torpedo tube.

Between the shadows of the two machine-guns, one on her

172

prow, the other on her transom, were the shapes of men, all facing forrard, all watching the sky. Four stood on the decking ahead of the hump of the rudimentary housing amidships; above the after end of the housing lay the raked windscreen, and there were two more crew in the well-deck abaft the housing. Six crew, and with a modicum of fortune, he reckoned, he could take them all within a minute.

Keeping submerged, surfacing silently and only for breath, he came astern of the boat, and up against its transom unobserved by any of the crew. The next moves had to be very quick. He lifted his arms out of the water, curled his fingers over the top edge of the transom, and took a grip. He placed one bare foot on top of the hanging rudder-guard, and then, sucking a quick, deep breath, he hoisted himself out of the sea and onto the stern decking.

The back end of the MTB dipped, rocking the long, narrow craft, and one of the men in her well-deck looked back. He saw the shape of the man there on the stern, and was puzzled by it, as Stallard's right hand wrapped tightly around the firing handle of the twelve-millimetre and swung the gun on its gimbals to aim forrard and his left hand, thumb and forefinger, gripped the cocking hammer and raked it back and knocked it forward.

Both hands now around the handles and his thumbs against the triggers, the ugly, stubby, air-cooled barrel in its perforated sleeve covering them all, he screamed at them:

'Get over or I'll blast you!'

The two in the well-deck went over rapidly, one on either side. Two of those on the decking forrard also went, crashing into the sea, leaving the boat rocking and splashing the bottom of her resin-bonded, moulded plywood hull against the waves of their entry. The water ran off Stallard's body into a pool on the deck at his feet. He shouted again at the two on the deck forrard. 'Get *over*!' and one of them went for the side and the other went for the twelve-millimetre on the prow; Stallard flicked his thumbs over the triggers and in that instant his gun fired ten bullets, practically all of which must have hit the man on the prow because you could see the fireworks flashing through him as he toppled backwards off the boat and hit the water.

Quickly now Stallard took a look into the south but saw nothing of the approaching *Shaheen*. It was 11.20, she was due five kilometres off the causeway within twenty-five minutes of now. He went ahead over the engine cowling and down into the cockpit. He began flicking switches on the control console until he found one that turned on the instrument panel lights; there were only two instruments, however, a big tachometer and an oil-pressure gauge. Then he found a knob that looked like a starter and gave it a pull. The engine roared once, coughed, stuttered, and roared again, and he reduced the revs to tickover while he went back astern and hauled in the anchor. From the ease with which it came up, he doubted that it had been on the bottom, let alone holding.

Back at the controls, he slipped the clutches in and the big boat began to move, lumbering at first and still low on the sea. He wanted to get the feel of her—he could not stop himself thinking of the boat as feminine—he wanted to get the feel of *it*. He was cruising her—*it*—now at just under two thousand revolutions, about ten knots, barely a quarter of her capacity, because he wanted to know how to manage this beast when he met the *Shaheen*. He tested a couple more switches and found her running lights, one on either side of her broad-splayed foredeck and one on the stern, and the switch for the big spotlight ahead of the windscreen. The light was mounted on a swivel and controlled with a handle that projected back through the glass.

On the port side, within reach of his left hand as he stood at the wheel, was a long lever to which for some moments he could assign no imaginable function. Then, seeing one exactly similar on the starboard side, he realised what they were—the torpedo firing levers.

Under the dash-panel was a radio-receiver-transmitter set, which must have been automatically switched on with the ignition.

174

Now that he had the layout of everything, he opened her up a little wider, pushing her to three thousand revs and swinging her in a long, easy turn about to head south. On an even, straight-ahead keel, he gave her full throttle. The giant Mercedes Benz engine, twenty-four cylinders in horizontally opposed banks of twelve, each squirting blue puffs of gas through its own private exhaust pipe, twelve, fat, sawn-off barrels in a row sticking out each side of the plywood hull just above the waterline, they all came awake with one tremendous, belly-trembling, lion-throated roar, and the big boat lifted its bows into the air and dug its tail into the smooth, warm sea and lit out south with the water rising in broad, lazily curving fans on either side of it. Within ten minutes, *Shaheen* was in sight on the horizon dead ahead.

It had to be *Shaheen*, for it was a fairly large boat and it was closing with him rapidly. Then, as the distance diminished, he recognised the configuration of her rigging lights, and knew for certain.

He put the phones on his ears and picked up the mike of the MTB's R/T set and pressed the button for transmit, hoping he had the right frequency and wave band. '*Shaheen*,' he signalled, 'this is Victor Stallard calling *Shaheen*, come in, *Shaheen*!'

Nothing came through the phones but crackle and static.

He called again. There was less than half a mile between them now and he wheeled off to starboard, swinging into a long circle to come back onto her port beam as she headed north.

The yacht was flying, her knife-sharp forefoot throwing up a bow-wave like a destroyer. She had to be within five kilometres of the bridge, and at this rate she would be there inside ten minutes.

After his third call, he got an answer.

He ordered the radio operator: 'Get Bazarki on the air!'

He was on the outer edge of the circumference of his circle now, coming around to head back at right angles to the yacht's line. She was a beautiful thing, white against the night, at speed, extended, and going like a skier down a long, smooth slope.

A voice came through the earphones: '*Shaheen* to Victor Stallard, come in Victor Stallard, over.'

He pressed the transmit button. 'Stallard, over.'

'Here is Mr Bazarki. Keep open.' There was crackling on the phones, and then a pop as they began receiving again, and Bazarki's voice, impatient, 'Stallard? Is that Victor Stallard? Over.'

'It is Victor Stallard,' he answered. 'I'm in the torpedo boat, off your port. I'm ordering you to go about, Jamil. You have five minutes, repeat, five minutes. If you haven't changed course within five minutes, I'm going to sink you. Over.'

'What are you saying, Stallard? Are you crazy? What has happened? Where is Colonel Davies? Where is Severin? Over.'

'Davies is dead,' Stallard said. 'Severin is not available for comment. I've told you what the score is. Your five minutes started one minute ago. I'm going off the air now. The time is eleven-fifty-seven. If you're not on the exact opposite heading by one minute after midnight, I'm going to torpedo you. Over and out.'

He switched off the set, stripped off the earphones, and dropped them with the mike onto the deck. The long, white yacht was now passing dead ahead of him. He swung ninety degrees north and ran parallel with her. Her speed remained steady and she showed no sign of turning. In the sky ahead, the pyrotechnics display above the causeway was already visible. He had to act; there were at least a thousand people on the causeway.

He put the wheel over hard to port and the boat practically stood on its transom, coming round, and as she straightened out his left hand was on the lever above the port torpedo tube. The helm steady, her bows aimed straight at the yacht, he started running in from about two thousand yards' range, the spotlight blazing across the water on the slim, white side of the *Shaheen*. Still she remained at full

176

ahead, without any sign of a course alteration. The time was midnight. One more minute. He turned the wheel again, describing another tight circle so as not to come too close to her. The yacht speared onward through the sea, no change at all to her course or speed.

They thought he was bluffing.

He grit his teeth, his heart pumping heavily and rapidly. Even in the back-rushing wind of the torpedo boat's slip-stream, he sweated now, his left hand tight on the torpedo lever.

12.01. He brought the boat back around, its bows aimed again for the yacht, running down on her from her port quarter. He let go the wheel and took the long iron lever in both hands, tightly, and shoved it forward.

The fish rushed from the tube and seemed to hang in the air, flying alongside the boat above the speeding sea, for seconds, and then dropped, belly-whacking the water, and racing ahead, barely submerged, leaving the boat behind, a flash of vicious silver like an attacking barracuda, marking out a long line pale as death across the surface towards the yacht.

Immediately the torpedo was gone, Stallard hauled the MTB off again and into another long, full circle, looking back at the yacht.

She was hit dead amidships. At first she just seemed to jump slightly in the sea. Then the whole waist of her erupted as a spout of water shot up through her and out the top of her and became a blossom of flame and a cloud of black smoke that enveloped the flame, and burst outwards, expanding. The dull, jarring crunch of the blast came a second after the flash, and then the yacht was lifted about the middle, her spine bending, her hull cracking, and then breaking, and she was in halves and visibly settling amidships.

As the MTB came around again, the yacht's bows were up, her prow pointing almost straight at the sky, and from further aft a mighty escalator of billowing, writhing black smoke was climbing away into the south. Her fuel tanks

177

had gone up. Those of her company as had survived the
blast were swarming like ants over her sides into the boiling
sea. He was not going to pick them up; there were more of
them than the MTB could conceivably accommodate, and
they would probably kill him anyway.

Shaheen's forrard section was settling fast, already two-
thirds of it were down. Her stern was going too, but more
sedately.

He turned the torpedo boat north, and ran for Jarma
Harbour.

14

As he swung in alongside the *Sandman*, Ali was standing
on the side-deck watching him, mystified. 'Sahib Vic?' he
asked, not prepared to trust his one eye in the darkness.

'Yes,' Stallard told him, then jumped aboard, bringing
a line from the torpedo boat. Then he heard a shout echoing round the cliff walls.

There was a group of people on Bazarki's wharf, Bimbo
Severin and the women. Severin was waving.

'Up anchor,' Stallard told Ali, and then went down into
the saloon and lifted the seat off the banquette. The nine-
millimetre Makarov was still there, wrapped in some oil
rags, with three loaded clips. Through the open port-hole
at head level he saw Ali's feet as the man passed forrard
along the side deck. 'Then start her up,' he called through
the port-hole, 'I'll be up in a minute.' He loaded the gun,
then went into the cabin and slipped off his wet shorts. He
put on a pair of jeans and put the Mak in the back pocket
of the jeans. The Mak, strangely, reminded him of the engineer on the *Shaheen*, Ali Makhoza—Scots-Jarmani; he
had been a good lad. There were probably several good
lads had gone down with the *Shaheen*.

The *Sandman*'s engines started up and rumbled away on tickover. He went on deck and crossed back to the MTB, climbing up onto its transom. Taking a grip on the twelve-millimetre, he swung it downwards and fired a long burst through the flimsy hull, opening a series of ragged holes through which the sea immediately gushed. Quickly, he jumped back to the *Sandman*, went up into the cockpit and let in her clutches, steering away from the sinking craft as Ali cast it off from the stern. He headed the *Sandman* in towards the wharf, a set of fairly intricate manœuvres, as there was a number of other craft moored around there. He hove-to about fifty feet off the wharf, from where he could see and hear Severin clearly.

'Bring them over, Bimbo,' he called. 'But leave your gun behind.'

The Russian grinned and shrugged and held up his open hands to indicate that he was unarmed. Then he helped the women down the steps from the wharf and into the dinghy that was tied up to the landing stage at the bottom. There were now four women—Godwin, who seemed to be rather drunk, Virginia and Sigrid Hasseler, and a blonde whom Stallard had never seen before. The blonde wore a dark shirt and tight, dark pants, and from Stallard's point of observation, she looked to be built the way blondes ought to be built. Trust bloody Bimbo, he thought.

The dinghy pulled into the side of the *Sandman* and Stallard had his hand ready on the butt of the gun in his hip pocket, just in case Severin did try to be clever. The Russian, however, merely helped the women climb up over the rail of the launch, and Stallard helped them from there on down, handing them back to Ali as they came aboard. 'Take them below,' he told the Arab. Then he looked down at Severin who remained standing in the dinghy, looking up at him and grinning.

'When I saw you dive off the terrace,' the Russian said, 'and I saw the MTB out there on the water, the crew gazing stupidly at the sky, I knew every move you were going to make. I saw the whole grande finale, the end of the Bee

Sting fiasco, in a flash in my mind like an inspiration. And you know something? For some inexplicable reason, my friend—as the Americans say—I was rooting for you.'

'Are you coming?' Stallard asked him.

'With you?'

'Why not?'

Severin shook his head and wanly smiled. 'That would mean defecting,' he said. 'A red Bolshevik bastard I may be, but I'm not a traitor. Thank you all the same. I have a sick submarine here, remember, that has to be got back home in one piece.'

Stallard grinned at him. He said, 'There's a job you and your submariners might like to do for Jarma before you leave. There's a live torpedo on the bottom of the harbour back there where I was moored.'

'We'll take care of it,' Severin said. Then he extended his right hand. 'Good luck, Vic,' he said. 'I hope we meet again.'

Shaking with him, Stallard said, 'I can't say it's been a pleasure, Bimbo; but I hope we meet again too.'

For some moments he stood in the well-deck, watching the big Russian set about rowing himself back to the wharf. He was lighting a much-needed cheroot when he remembered the blonde who had come aboard.

'Bimbo!' he shouted.

The Russian stopped rowing and looked back.

'Your blonde,' Stallard called.

Severin said, 'Oh yes,' and turned the dinghy around and with a couple of pulls on the oars brought himself back. He spoke quietly, clinging to the gunwale of the launch. 'La Diablesse,' he said. 'The black hair was a wig.'

'You left us between about six and eight o'clock this evening,' Stallard said. 'Is that where you were?'

The Russian grinned and shrugged. 'They were not all virgins after all,' he said. 'Au'voir!' And he set out rowing for the wharf again. He turned just once more, to call softly across the water, 'She is known in London, I understand, as Mrs Black!'

180

Stallard went down into the saloon. Godwin was lying on the settee moaning and Ali was serving coffee. Sigrid Hasseler sat on the end of the settee with Godwin's feet behind her, and Virginia Hasseler stood by the hi-fi console against the forrard bulkhead. The blonde woman stood alone, on the port side, gazing fixedly through an open porthole, watching Bimbo Severin going ashore. For a moment, Stallard looked at her, but she did not look round, so he shifted his eyes to Virginia Hasseler. The preceding twelve hours had been rough with her and she looked to be suffering slightly from shock. She was trembling and pale in the face and her eyes were sunken, and ringed darkly.

Stallard said, 'We're pushing off now. I should get some sleep.'

Then he went back up into the cockpit and reversed the *Sandman* out of the area of moored boats and turned her for the harbour heads. Ali came up and offered to take the wheel, but Stallard told him to go and bed down for a few hours. It would take a few hours for Stallard's nerves to settle sufficiently to allow him to sleep.

The *Sandman* stood out from the dark bulk of Jarma Island under a great, anaemic moon, upon a sea of the texture and hue of a sheet of stainless steel. Gulf nights are very beautiful and in the middle of this one Stallard sat in the high-chair behind the wheel, sucking on a long, black cheroot by the dull green glow off the compass rose, occasionally swigging from a bottle of rhum Negrita which he housed in a locker ahead of the binnacle. Below, the light in the saloon was switched off, and shortly after that the door opened and Mrs Black came up the three stairs into the cockpit. For a while she stood in silence beside him, staring straight ahead through the glass, at the sea.

Then she said, 'You know who I am?'

'Yes,' he said.

'Miss Godwin told you about me?'

'Yes.'

'Virginia Hasseler knows—or has guessed,' she said,

'but the girl does not know. I would be obliged if it stayed that way.'

'Yes,' Stallard said, again. 'Yes, of course.'

Then the woman said, 'No good purpose would be served by telling her at this time of her life.'

Stallard sucked his cheroot and offered her the rum bottle. 'Want a pull?'

The bottle threw her for a moment; she looked at it, and then said, 'No, thank you,' and then looked at him, strangely intrigued.

'Tell me about La Diablesse, Mrs Black,' Stallard said. 'How did she come to be in Bazarki's floor-show?'

The woman said, 'I have an interest in the company that controls the agency that has a branch in Beirut through which Bazarki booked the performers. They told me he wanted a stripper, and they very kindly allowed La Diablesse to fill that slot. I wanted to be here because—well, as you probably know, Cynthia Godwin phoned me from Bahrain and told me that Virginia Hasseler was going to take Sigrid to Jarma for the causeway inauguration ceremoney; Cynthia also told me that you didn't feel that that was wise. So I decided to be here.'

'And why did you assassinate Colonel Davies?'

'I saw Davies this afternoon with Bimbo Severin. I had photographs of Davies taken in London when he was trying to get at me—he, of course, didn't recognise me, but I knew him. So I waited until they had parted, and then I approached Severin. We talked, and—well—we talked. You know Bimbo Severin.'

'Yes.' Stallard grinned.

'He told me he would bring you all down to watch the show. And he told me that Stallard—you—would probably appreciate it very much if I could arrange for some kind of a diversion to occur. He didn't actually tell me you were in trouble. That was all he would say, and he wouldn't elaborate. But when I saw Davies standing by you, and the two with the machine-guns, I understood what he

182

meant. So I decided I had better start thinking about this diversion, and I think the one that I came up with was rather successful, wasn't it? It gave me great pleasure to put that knife into Davies' throat. He murdered Tod Spencer, who was a man to whom I owed a great deal.'

Stallard recalled his conversation with the Russian at the party on the terrace of Bazarki's house the previous morning. 'I might be able to get you out of this alive,' Severin had said. Even then he had been thinking about it; and the scene in the room upstairs that had followed—that must have decided him—cold stone sober the bastard had offered to marry Godwin! Stallard was almost laughing out loud at the recollection. But the Russian had been torn between personal feeling and moral duty; and allegiance to the hammer and sickle had been fed into that hard-eyed Bolshevik with his mother's milk. He could not possibly have helped them escape in person. He had just dropped a veiled hint to Mrs Black.

'Thank God you were there, anyway,' Stallard said softly to the woman.

'You did pretty well yourself, Mr Stallard,' she said, and looked at him and grinned. 'Good night.'

'Good night,' he said.

She went down the steps into the saloon, and the door closed behind her.

Just before dawn, Ali came up and took over the wheel and Stallard went down into the saloon. Godwin was stretched out, fully clothed and quite unconscious, on the settee. The Hasseler girls and Mrs Black must have been sharing the cabin forrard. He lit a cigarette and sat on the edge of the settee, and Godwin stirred and moaned.

'How do you feel?' he asked her.

'Turn that bloody engine off,' she whispered.

'We'll be in Bahrain in half an hour.'

'Give me a cigarette then.'

He lit a cigarette and gave it to her.

'What's going to happen now?' she asked him.

'I was thinking,' he said. 'I could just use a couple of

weeks down in Angola helping old Heini chase that elephant out of his pineapple patch.'

'Oh yes?' Godwin said.

'Well,' he said, 'Mrs Voltz did make me promise to come back when this was all over and tell them how it worked out. I think old Heini would like to know.'

'You also think that there might be five thousand dollars in a bank in Luanda, deposited by Bazarki in the name of Victor Stallard,' she said.

'Good God!' he said. 'I'd forgotten all about that.'

'You're a bastard, Stallard,' she told him.

'Why do you damn women always have to look for a mercenary motive behind everything?' he asked her.

'Because, my darling,' she said, 'when it comes to men, there usually is one. Fix me a drink.'